ACCOLADES FOR THE
ALDO ZELNICK COMIC NOVEL SERIES

An alphabetical series for middle-grade readers 7 to 13

2009 Book of the Year Award, juvenile fiction, *ForeWord Reviews*

2010 Colorado Book Award, juvenile literature

2010 Mountains & Plains Independent Booksellers
Association Regional Book Award

2010 *Creative Child* magazine Seal of Excellence

2010 Next Generation Indie Book Award finalist

Winter 2010 Kids' Next Indiebound selection

2011 CYBIL nomination

WHAT READERS ARE SAYING:

(kid comments are in Aldo's handwriting)

"It was the funniest book I have ever read. The illustrations are hilarious. It is better than Diary of a Wimpy Kid."

- Tavis

"Greg Heffley and Ellie McDoodle, move over–Aldo Zelnick is here!"

— Mary Lee Hahn, teacher and readingyear.blogspot.com blogger

"*Bogus* is just as fantastic as *Artsy-Fartsy*. The humor and creativity are amazing, and my son LOVES this series about Aldo. We are all looking forward to the next books. Keep them coming!"

— Katie Maguire

"This is a book that definitely speaks 'kid speak.' The first installment in an A-to-Z Series, *Artsy-Fartsy* is perfect for reluctant readers. It's fun for kids and will be appreciated by parents and teachers for the amusing 'back door' approach to enriching vocabulary. Look out Wimpy Kid!"

— Stacy Morris, Katy Budget Books, Houston, TX

"I REALLY LIKED YOUR ARTSY-FARTSY BOOK. I WOULD PUT IT ON MY TOP 10 LIST."

- Zach

"The other night I caught my 8-year-old twins giggling on the living room couch as they took turns reading *Artsy-Fartsy* aloud to each other. Then one morning I found it on their nightstand with a headlamp resting on the cover from the previous night's under-cover reading. That's a true badge of honor in this house. You hit this one out of the park."

- Becky Jensen

"We talk about the book Bogus at school because it is so cool. I really like it."
- Yisel

"One of the most remarkable things about these books is the voice of Aldo, which rings true from every page. The hilarious drawings enhance the text with jokes and visual humor that make Aldo's personality pop."
— Rebecca McGregor, Picture Literacy

"THE BOOK WAS VERY HILARIOUS. IT MADE US LAUGH OUT LOUD. YOU HAVE THE BEST CHARACTERS EVER!"
- Sebastian

"Visually stimulating and cleverly academic... Young readers will enjoy the wit and humor of main character Aldo Zelnick."
— *ForeWord Reviews*

"Artsy-Fartsy is the best book I have ever read. It is a very hilarious book."
- Mattias

"*Bogus* is the second graphic novel featuring the irrepressible Aldo Zelnick, kid detective and linguist extraordinaire. Aldo is a great hero for kids because he is exactly that: another believable kid. Pretty wonderful when you stop to examine him, after all. The comic illustrations keep the pages turning, as does the fast-moving story. Kids will love to collect all the letters of the alphabet as discovered by Aldo Zelnick."

— *Midwest Book Review*

"My students and I are really enjoying *Artsy-Fartsy*. I think the children can identify with Aldo. I introduced *Artsy-Fartsy* to the other fourth grade grammar and composition teacher, and she has used the book as well. We like to use good literature in our teaching, and this year we used *Artsy-Fartsy* to emphasize 'voice' to our students. We also asked the students to identify thoughts and emotions used in the story. We are looking forward to the continuing adventures of Aldo, his friends and family."

- Carol Gorman, 4th grade teacher

"My class and I loved Artsy-Fartsy. It was the best book of 3rd grade."

- Tanner

"I am completely charmed by this series. The drawings and text have the quality of simultaneously being appealing to children and also amusing for adults. A big strength here is in the development of the characters. This is wonderful, since this is going to be an A to Z series and we'll have plenty of time to get to know them better. These are individuals with staying power. With the sketchbook comes a wonderful, not-overstated message of allowing Aldo to be himself and follow his creativity. Bravo!"

- Jean Hanson

"As was the case in the first book, *Bogus* is filled with so much humor as well as terrific illustrations. The reader once again has the opportunity to see what a great (and funny) character Aldo is. There is also a bit of a mystery to solve as well as some important lessons. I especially like that *Bogus* features many "B" words and has a "B Gallery" in the back of the book that gives definitions. I am excited to say that there is another Aldo book in the works called *Cahoots*. If it's anything like the first two books, then it's guaranteed to be not only funny but also very educational. What a terrific mix for kids and their parents!"

— Julie Peterson, Booking Mama book reviewer

Cahoots

AN ALDO ZELNICK COMIC NOVEL

Written by Karla Oceanak

Illustrated by Kendra Spanjer

BAILIWICK PRESS

*Also by Karla Oceanak
and Kendra Spanjer —*
Artsy-Fartsy
Bogus

Published by:
Bailiwick Press
309 East Mulberry Street
Fort Collins, Colorado 80524
(970) 672-4878
Fax: (970) 672-4731
www.bailiwickpress.com
www.aldozelnick.com

Manufactured by:
Friesens Corporation, Altona, Canada
February 2011
Job # 63749

Book design by:
Launie Parry
Red Letter Creative
www.red-letter-creative.com

ISBN 978-1-934649-08-4

Library of Congress Control Number: 2010941365

20 19 18 17 16 15 14 13 12 11   7 6 5 4 3 2 1

Dear Aldo -
Your cartoons are
the cat's pajamas.*
Keep them coming!
Sloppy kisses,
Goosy
XOXOXOXOX

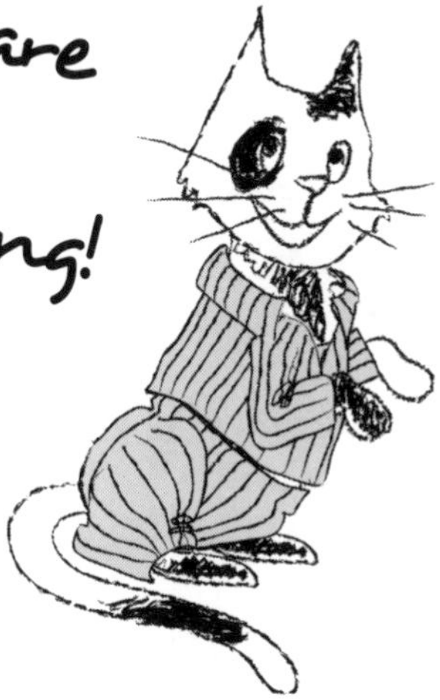

ALDO,

oh say can you C?

(I'm confident* you can.)

Mr. Mot

WHO'S WHO

TIMOTHY, MY BROTHER. ATHLETIC, COMPETITIVE,* UBER-TEXTER.

ME—ALDO ZELNICK. LOVES GAMEBOY. LOVES GAMEBOY WITH CHOCOLATE DOUGHNUTS EVEN MORE.

MY MOM, CLAIRE ZELNICK. BIRD-WATCHER, TECHNOLOGY-HATER, CONNIPTION*-HAVER.

GOOSY, MY GRANDMA. PERMANENT SMILER.

MAX. BEST DOG EVER.

MY DAD, LEO ZELNICK. I GET MY LOVE OF FOOD—AND MY HAIR—FROM HIM.

MY COMIC'S CHARACTERS: LETTUCE LADY, BACON BOY, AND TORMADO.

↳ MY CAGEY* COUSINS, CHAZ AND AL.

AUNT CAROLINE. GOOD AT MAKING BUTTER. AND ACTING.

GRANDMA AND GRANDPA ANDERSON— SQUARES. I MEAN, SQUARE DANCERS.

UNCLE ODIN—MY MOM'S BROTHER AND TERRIBLE FIDDLE PLAYER.

MR. MOT. MY ↑ WORD-NERD NEIGHBOR.

↑ BEE. GOOD DRAWER AND FORT HANGER-OUTER.

↳ JACK. MY BEST FRIEND SINCE FOREVER.

9

(My name is Aldo. This is the third sketchbook my grandma Goosy has given me. If you haven't already, you might want to read the first one, *Artsy-Fartsy*, to find out how this whole alphabetical sketchbook thing got started. Oh, and whenever you see this *, you can look in the Word Gallery at the end of the book to see what the word means.)

How AM I EVER SUPPOSED TO ACHIEVE MY FULL GAMING POTENTIAL WITH ALL THESE DISTRACTIONS?

HOME, e-HOME

Today Mom had a colossal* conniption.*

I was minding my own business, playing a computer game with one eye and watching TV with the other, and my brother, Timothy, was texting, as usual, when Mom interrupted us with her vacuuming.

Couldn't she see we were concentrating?

Finally she turned off the vacuum and put her hands on her hips. In mom body-language, that is <u>never</u> a good sign.

"You boys have had <u>2</u> <u>full</u> <u>months</u> of summer vacation to lounge," she said. "Clean your rooms, <u>right now</u>, then go OUTSIDE and get some FRESH AIR. No more electronics today. I'm going to the store, and when I get home, I'll need your help putting the groceries away. In a family, everyone has to contribute.*"

Ugh.

So, I went up to my room and fed Bogus, my bodacious betta fish. I neatly balled up my bedspread and pushed my pajamas under my pillow. As I looked around, I noticed a couple things scattered on the floor, so I nudged them under the bed with my foot. There. Room clean.

Then, because I <u>always</u> do what
my mom tells me to do, I
stepped out of the house and
was nearly blinded by the
sun. Sheesh it's bright
OUTSIDE. I ambled to our
fort under the giant pine
tree, where my friends Jack and
Bee were playing Crazy Eights. I
lay down on the fort futon, pulled
my GameBoy out of my pocket,
and conquered* a few Mario levels.

IF OUR SUN IS
A STAR, HOW
COME IT SHINES
DURING THE DAY
AND DISAPPEARS
AT NIGHT?

"Want to play cards with us, Aldo?" asked
Bee. "We'll deal you in."

"Nah," I said. "I need to focus."

Eventually I went home for a snack. Dad and Timothy were watching TV, so I grabbed the laptop to play Farm Town. It's an online game where you make a little farmer who looks like you, then farmer-you plants seeds and harvests crops and stuff like that. It's pretty authentic.

I'm level 18 now, so I'm a Master Farmer. I have a farmhouse, a giant garden, chickens and a rooster, cows, and lots more farmish stuff. My goal is level 59—Zenith Farmer. That's when you can get a swimming pool, because really, what's a farm without a swimming pool?

One farm lesson I've learned the hard way is to ALWAYS hire other people to harvest your crops. It's way too much work to do it yourself! All that clicking makes your arm sore. Raspberries are the best crop—but if you don't harvest them a few hours after planting, they shrivel up and die. So you have to play at least 5 or 6 times a day.

I was so caught up in my farm chores that I didn't even hear Mom come in, but for some reason I looked up, and there she was.

"Oh good, I'm <u>starving</u>," I said to her. "What's for dinner?"

HELLOOO! I AM NOT A DIGITAL IMAGE! I AM AN ACTUAL HUMAN BEING STANDING HERE IN THE FLESH TRYING TO COMMUNICATE WITH YOU! TIMOTHY AND ALDO, I SAID <u>NO MORE</u> ELECTRONICS TODAY! REMEMBER THAT?! DID YOU CLEAN YOUR ROOMS?! DID YOU GO OUTSIDE ON THIS BEAUTIFUL DAY AND GET SOME FRESH AIR?! DID YOU EVEN TAKE POOR MAX FOR A WALK?!! YOU ARE WASTING YOUR LIVES WITH THESE COCKAMAMIE* MACHINES!!!!!!!!!!!!!!!!!!

BUT I'VE BEEN LEARNING HOW TO BE A FARMER!

YEAH. WHAT SHE SAID.

SHE <u>IS</u> RIGHT. BUT SHE'S ALSO BLOCKING MY VIEW OF THE CRICKET MATCH.

15

"Welp, looks like we're cooking tonight, kids," said Dad. "Let's get started."

While we made dinner, Mom took Max for an uber-long walk. When she got back, she was all smiley, which made me suspicious. She pulled my dad aside, and they had a whispered conversation. Then during dessert, she announced that her brother, my Uncle Odin, had invited us to his farm in Minnesota for an old-fashioned summer vacation.

LEO ZELNICK'S CHICKEN SALAD

IT'S A CARNIVORE'S* SALAD WITH NO LEAFY GREEN-NESS! YESSS!

- CUT-UP COOKED CHICKEN
- DRIED CRANBERRIES—LOTS
- CHOPPED CELERY, GREEN ONIONS, & PECANS
- MAYO TO MAKE IT STICK TOGETHER
- SALT & PEPPER
- NO LETTUCE

"We're going to stay with your aunt and uncle and cousins on the farm where I grew up!" Mom said. "You are going to love it. Just think...a full week of FRESH AIR and living off the land!"

Farm Town in real life? That sounds like a terrible idea. We leave in 3 days.

FORTITUDE

"We're going clothes shopping," Mom said first thing this morning. "You need new underwear for the trip—and also some school clothes. School starts a few days after we get back from Minnesota!"

Why are moms so insensitive sometimes?

I had just woken up, for Pete's sake, and not only was she talking to me, she was stringing a bunch of appalling information together:

1. I had to go clothes shopping.
2. She wanted to buy me new underwear (embarrassing!).
3. My last, precious days of summer vacation would be spent OUTSIDE, far away from my friends.
4. Summer vacation is almost over.

I did a quick mental calculation* and decided I only had the power to change 1 of the 4 cruel* realities. I took a stand.

"Nope," I said. "I'm not going shopping."

"So you're saying you like your ratty old underwear."

"Yep."

"And you don't care what you'll have to wear to school a couple weeks from now."

"Nope."

Mom put her hands on her hips, so I put my hands on my hips. If we were going to have a showdown, I had to look like a contender.*

THE CLOTHES I HAVE ARE COMPLETELY FINE.

OK, MISTER, YOU'LL JUST HAVE TO WEAR WHAT I PICK OUT.

GOOD JOB, ALDO. KEEP DISTRACTING MOM SO SHE DOESN'T GET ON MY CASE.

It seemed my calm, cool, and collected*
attitude worked. Timothy, who actually cares
how he looks, went shopping with Mom and my
grandma, Goosy, while I got to go chillax* in the
fort with Jack and Bee. I told them about the trip
to the farm.

"Wow, Aldo. I bet they have an amazing
vegetable garden," said Bee, whose favorite part of
the grocery store is the produce section. "I wish I
could see it."

"That's dumb," Jack and I said.

"Actually, the vitamins in veggies make you
smarter," said Bee.

"Have you ever been to this farm?" asked
Jack. He had kind of a weird look on his face.

"We went there once or twice when I was
little," I said. "I don't remember it, but I've seen the
pictures of me petting a cow and stuff."

Then Jack handed me a little flashlight thing
with a strap. "I thought you might want to
borrow my headlamp...for your trip," he said. "You
never know when you might not have electricity."

19

"Uhhh...okaaay," I said.

"How old are your cousins?" asked Bee.

"They're a couple years older. They're twins.
Hey, Jack, will you feed Bogus while I'm gone?"

"Sure. Who's taking care of Max?"

"He's gonna stay with Mr. Mot."

"Oh."

Then we slurped our Slushies in silence.

Later on, the shoppers came home, and that's when I learned that there is something worse than clothes shopping: having your annoyed mom, your evil brother, and your kooky grandmother pick out clothes for you.

They did bring me chocolate-covered cherries from the candy store at the mall, but to get them I had to model the clothes they'd bought for me. It was so unfair.

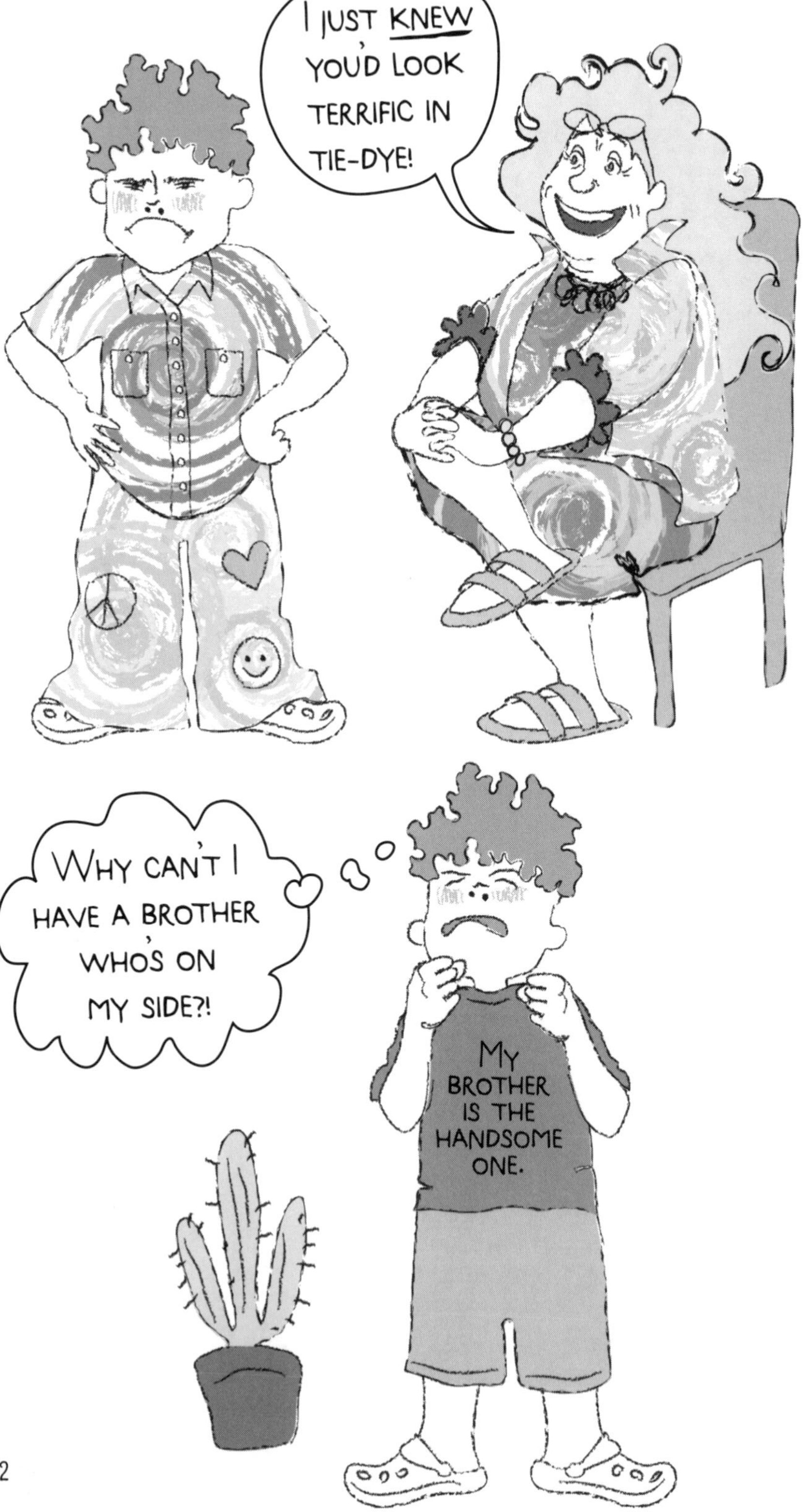
I JUST KNEW YOU'D LOOK TERRIFIC IN TIE-DYE!
WHY CAN'T I HAVE A BROTHER WHO'S ON MY SIDE?!
MY BROTHER IS THE HANDSOME ONE.

And, as if the fashion show wasn't embarrassing enough...my mom also bought me the dorkiest underwear in the history of underwear. There's NO way I'm wearing them.

CIAO*

Welp, we left. We got in the car, and we drove away from the only home I've ever known.

Even though it was early morning, Goosy and our neighbor, Mr. Mot, came to see us off.

"You are about to have an audacious adventure, Aldo," said Goosy as she clambered* onto the roof of the minivan.

"The world is a book, and those who don't travel read only one page," said Mr. Mot, who had stuffed his pockets with dog treats for Max.

Dad hummed while he plugged his iPod into the minivan's radio. "Wait till you hear the playlists I've prepared!" he said.

Mom smiled as she showed me the cooler she'd packed with healthy snacks (ew) for the ride.

Mom was happy. Dad was happy. Goosy and Mr. Mot were happy. Even Max was happy. I started to feel a blip of happiness too. After all, we were going on a vacation!

(And Timothy? He was sleeping, as he usually is before noon. He sleepwalked out to the car and immediately lay down in the backseat. I don't think he even opened his eyes.)

Goosy climbed down from the top of the car, and she and Mr. Mot and Maxie waved goodbye. As we drove away, I asked Mom to hand me the laptop. *Might as well pop in a movie,* I thought.

"We didn't bring the computer, Aldo," she said blithely. "But I brought car bingo!"

"What?! No computer!" I said. *Oh well.* I reached into my backpack for my GameBoy, but I couldn't feel it. I pulled the backpack onto my lap, unzipped it, and searched carefully. "Hey, where's my GameBoy? I packed it last night!"

"I took that out, sport," said Dad. "We're going to remember how to have fun <u>without</u> electronics on this trip."

*Oh no, it's a conspiracy.** "But <u>you</u> brought your iPod!" I said.

"True. But just so we can enjoy music together on the car ride."

"And audiobooks!" chimed in Mom. "I downloaded the complete *Little House on the Prairie* collection for us to listen to!"

So here I am, stuck beside healthy snacks, smelly feet, and not <u>one</u> battery-operated device to keep me occupied for the next thousand miles.

<u>This cannot be happening!</u>

I'm going to work on my Bacon Boy comic strip, which I invented in my last sketchbook. (Bacon Boy and his friends are superheroes.)

Maybe that'll make me feel better.

BACON BOY in "I GOTTA GO."

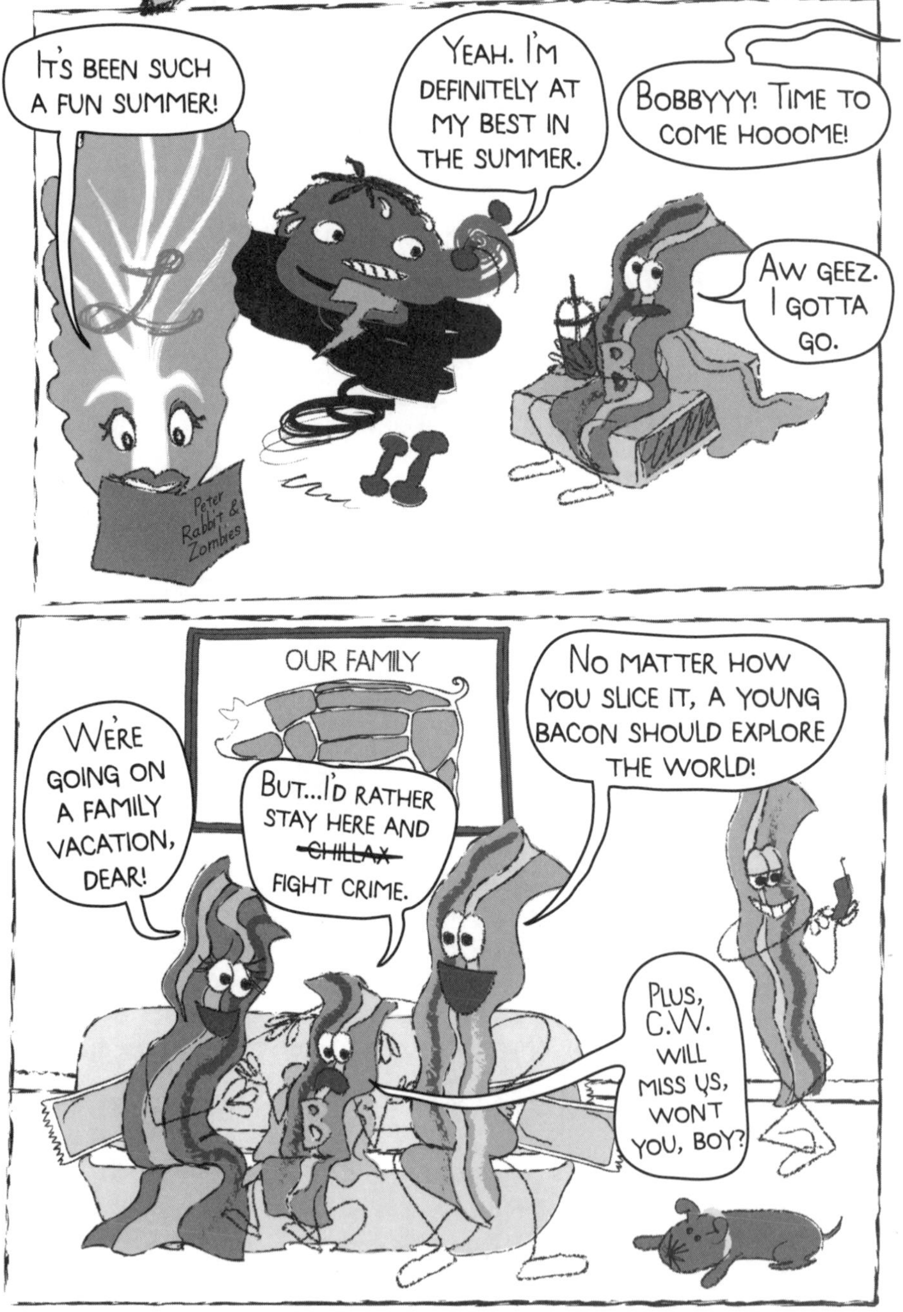
IT'S BEEN SUCH A FUN SUMMER!
YEAH. I'M DEFINITELY AT MY BEST IN THE SUMMER.
BOBBYYY! TIME TO COME HOOOME!
AW GEEZ. I GOTTA GO.
Peter Rabbit & Zombies
OUR FAMILY
WE'RE GOING ON A FAMILY VACATION, DEAR!
BUT...I'D RATHER STAY HERE AND ~~CHILLAX~~ FIGHT CRIME.
NO MATTER HOW YOU SLICE IT, A YOUNG BACON SHOULD EXPLORE THE WORLD!
PLUS, C.W. WILL MISS US, WONT YOU, BOY?

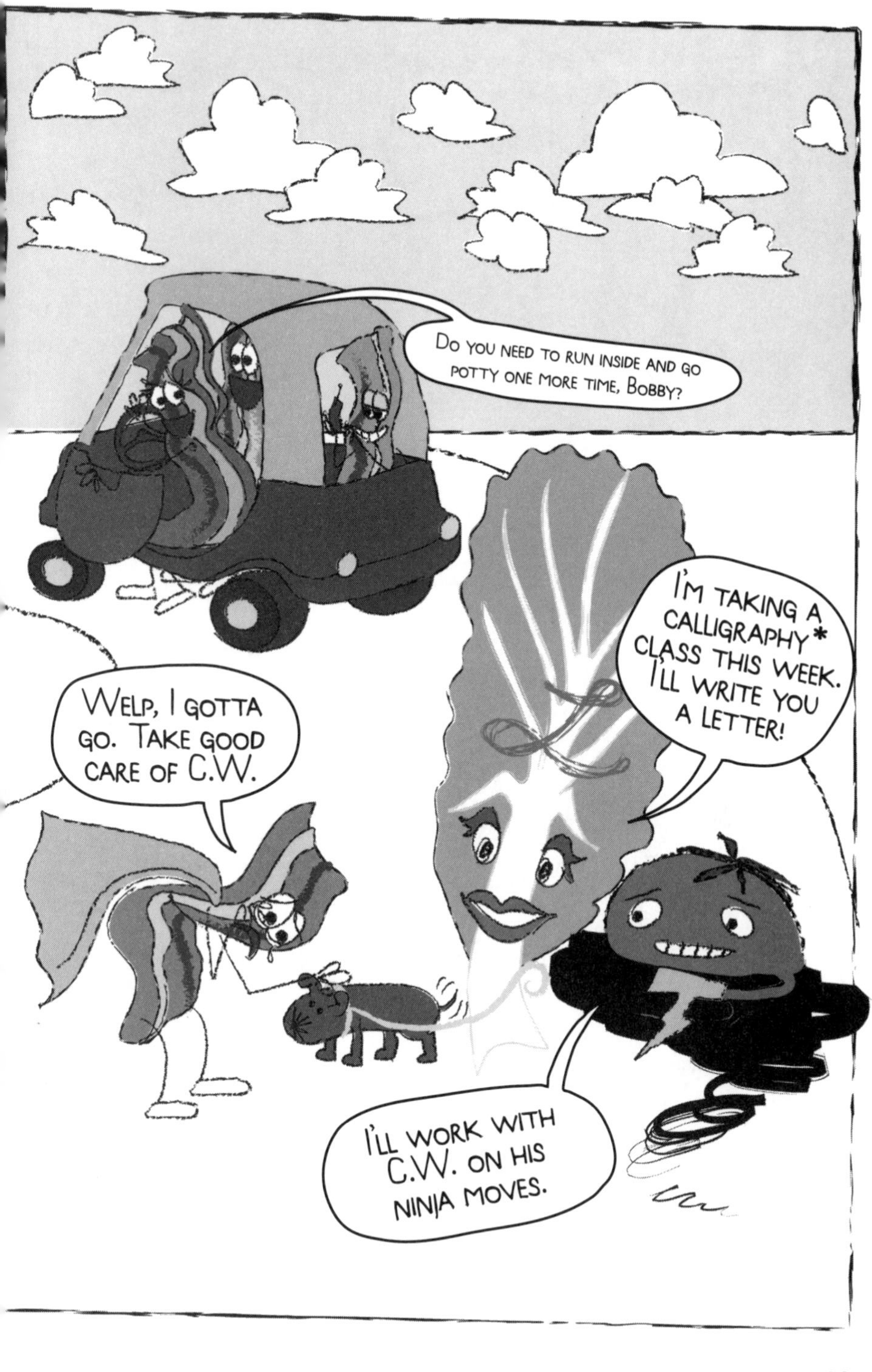
Do you need to run inside and go potty one more time, Bobby?
I'm taking a calligraphy* class this week. I'll write you a letter!
Welp, I gotta go. Take good care of C.W.
I'll work with C.W. on his ninja moves.

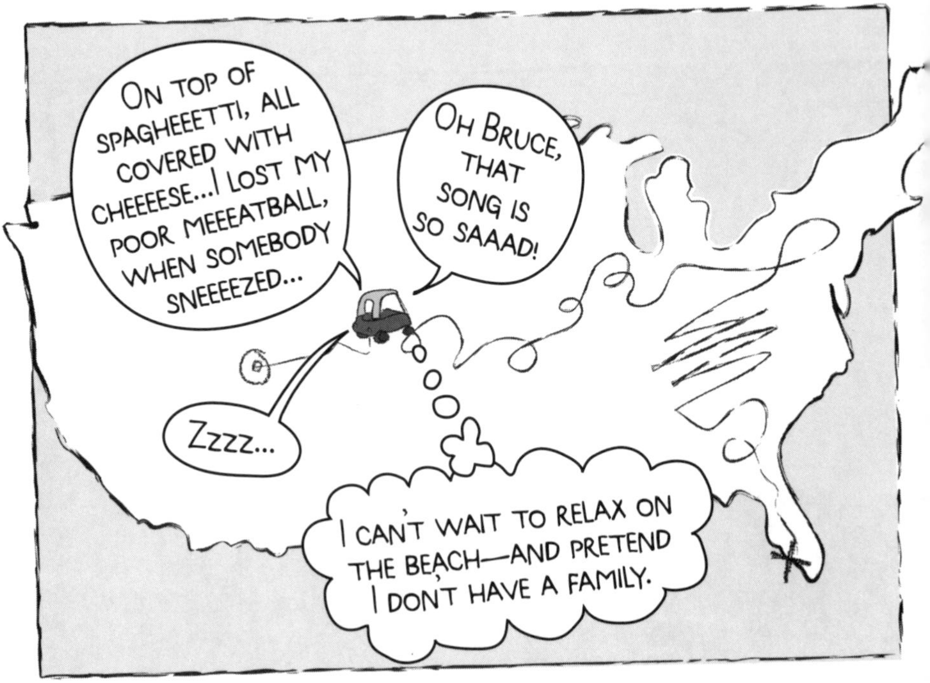
ON TOP OF SPAGHEEETTI, ALL COVERED WITH CHEEEESE...I LOST MY POOR MEEEATBALL, WHEN SOMEBODY SNEEEEZED...
OH BRUCE, THAT SONG IS SO SAAAD!
ZZZZ...
I CAN'T WAIT TO RELAX ON THE BEACH—AND PRETEND I DON'T HAVE A FAMILY.

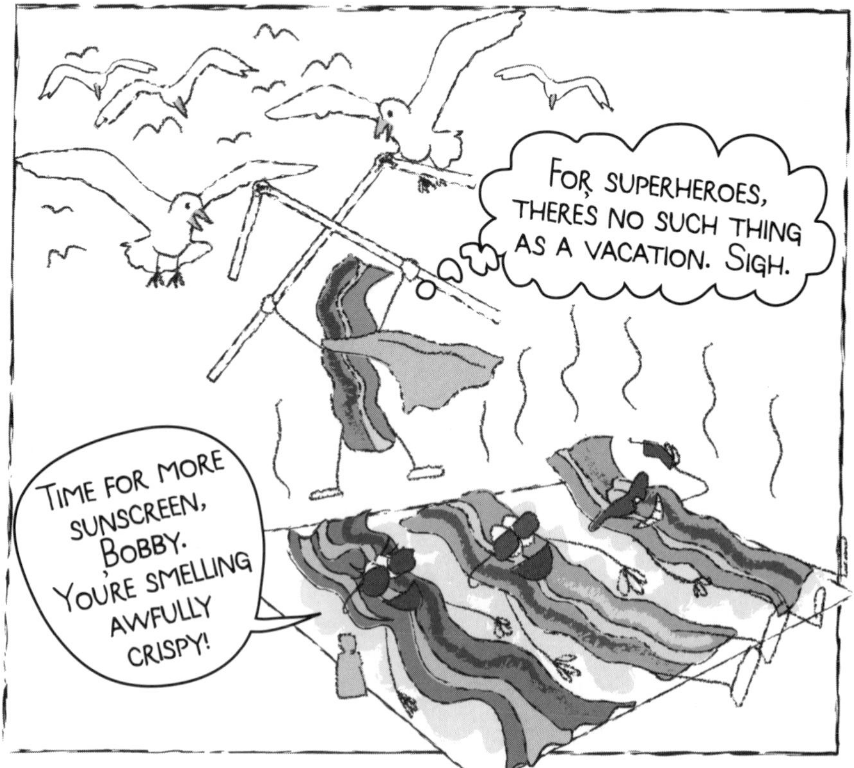
FOR SUPERHEROES, THERE'S NO SUCH THING AS A VACATION. SIGH.
TIME FOR MORE SUNSCREEN, BOBBY. YOU'RE SMELLING AWFULLY CRISPY!

THE SOUTH DAKOTA TRAIL

We've been in the car for a few hours now. Mostly I've been in shock, after learning that we'd be traveling like cavemen, with no modern conveniences.*

No ELECTRONICS FOR 30,000 MORE YEARS? I'M BORED.

My Bacon Boy strip is looking pretty good, but who knew Mr. and Mrs. Bacon would be so coldhearted?* They're going to give baconkind a bad name.

After a while Mom handed me a cup of cut-up cantaloupe* and a toothpick to eat it with.

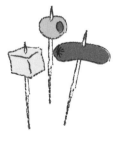

Hmmm. Why is it that food that's good for you actually TASTES GOOD when you eat it with a toothpick? Whoa...I just realized: ALL food that's toothpicked is delicious. (Note to self: Copyright* this idea.)

"OK, so how long is this trip, anyway?"
I asked, snapping out of my catatonic* state. "Will
we be there in time for me to harvest the cabbage
I planted last night on my Farm Town farm?"

My dad chortled.* "We've got a full day
of road-trip fun ahead of us." He handed me the
atlas, which had a squiggly line drawn across four
states.

"A full day?" I complained. "That's FOREVER!"

"It'll fly by, Aldo—I promise. Prepare to be
amazed."

(Hmph. What would amaze me would be a
portable DVD player falling from the sky into my
lap. But since I'm stuck in the car, I guess copying
the atlas is the best entertainment I've got.)

WE STARTED HERE, IN "COLORFUL COLORADO"...

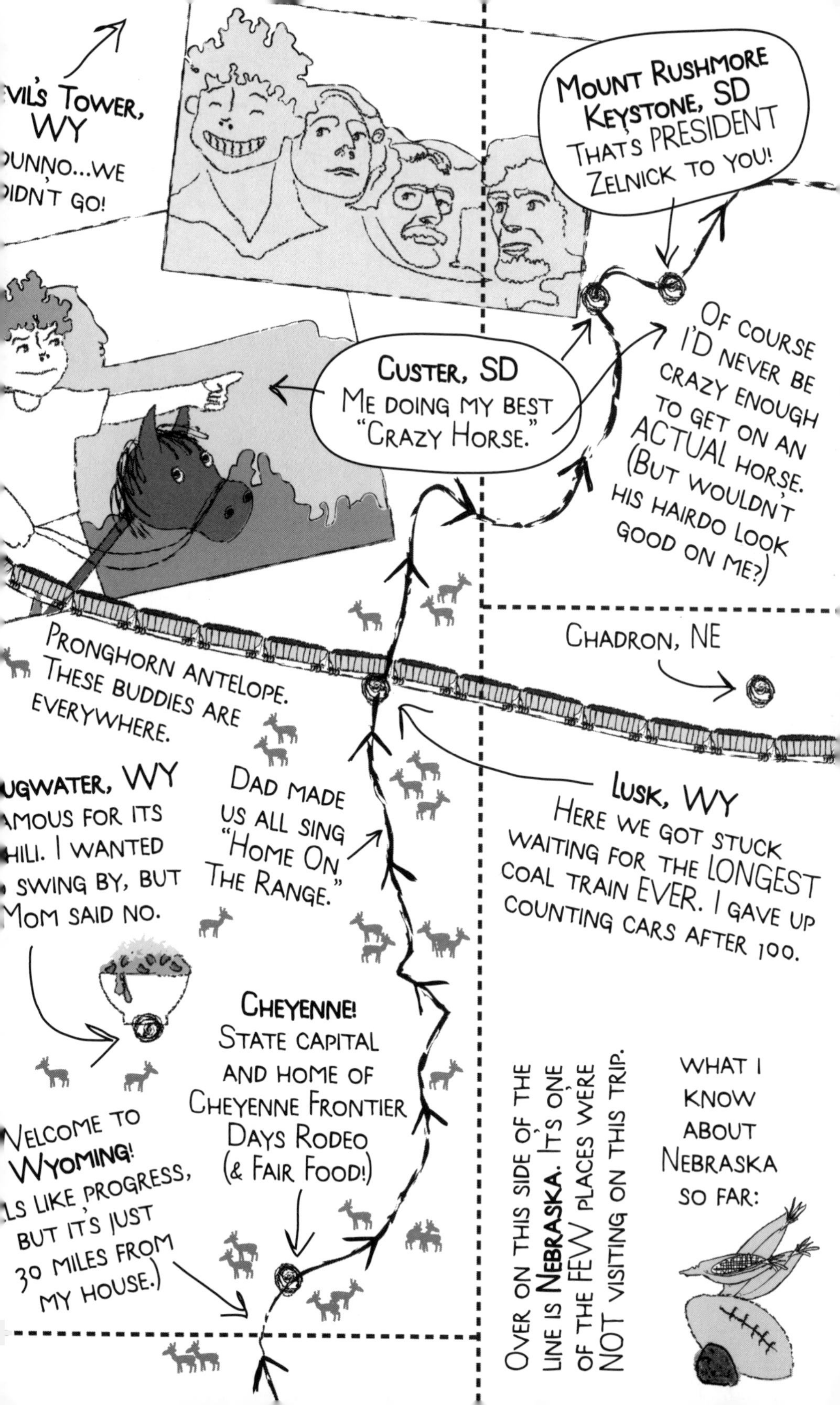

EVIL'S TOWER, WY
DUNNO...WE DIDN'T GO!
MOUNT RUSHMORE KEYSTONE, SD
THAT'S PRESIDENT ZELNICK TO YOU!
CUSTER, SD
ME DOING MY BEST "CRAZY HORSE."
OF COURSE I'D NEVER BE CRAZY ENOUGH TO GET ON AN ACTUAL HORSE. (BUT WOULDN'T HIS HAIRDO LOOK GOOD ON ME?)
CHADRON, NE
PRONGHORN ANTELOPE. THESE BUDDIES ARE EVERYWHERE.
UGWATER, WY
AMOUS FOR ITS HILI. I WANTED SWING BY, BUT MOM SAID NO.
DAD MADE US ALL SING "HOME ON THE RANGE."
LUSK, WY
HERE WE GOT STUCK WAITING FOR THE LONGEST COAL TRAIN EVER. I GAVE UP COUNTING CARS AFTER 100.
CHEYENNE!
STATE CAPITAL AND HOME OF CHEYENNE FRONTIER DAYS RODEO (& FAIR FOOD!)
VELCOME TO WYOMING!
LS LIKE PROGRESS, BUT IT'S JUST 30 MILES FROM MY HOUSE.)
OVER ON THIS SIDE OF THE LINE IS NEBRASKA. IT'S ONE OF THE FEW PLACES WERE NOT VISITING ON THIS TRIP.
WHAT I KNOW ABOUT NEBRASKA SO FAR:

WE'RE STILL IN **SOUTH DAKOTA**. CAN YOU BELIEVE IT?

THIS IS WHERE MOM STARTED PLAYING THE *LITTLE HOUSE IN THE BIG WOODS* AUDIOBOOK ON THE CAR RADIO. IT'S ABOUT SOME GIRL WHO LIVED IN A LOG CABIN IN THE PIONEER DAYS AND ALL THE EXCITING THINGS SHE GOT TO DO, LIKE PLAY WITH CORNCOB DOLLS AND BALLOONS MADE FROM PIGS' BLADDERS. TIMOTHY PUT A PILLOW OVER HIS HEAD AND FELL BACK ASLEEP.

MURDO, SD
CAR MUSEUM (COOL!) AND SWITCH TO CENTRAL TIME ZONE. DAD SAYS THIS MEANS WE LOSE AN HOUR. I THINK WE'VE LOST WAY MORE THAN THAT BY NOW.

WALL DRUG
(**WALL, SD**)
THIS IS THE PLACE WE'VE BEEN SEEING A BILLION SIGNS FOR THIS WHOLE TIME.

Zz

HAVE YOU DUG WALL DRUG?

AND WHAT'S NOT TO DIG? COOL SOUVENIRS, BUFFALO BURGERS, FRESH DOUGHNUTS, AND A BEHEMOTH JACKALOPE STATUE YOU CAN SIT ON.

JACKALOPE = JACKRABBIT + ANTELOPE

WALL DRUG

DOWN HERE IS MORE **NEBRASKA**.

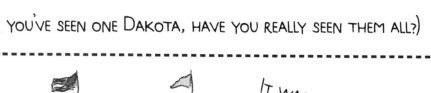

IT WAS A-MAIZE-ING!!!

MINNESOTA!
(FINALLY!)

ENTERING
THE LAND OF
10,000 LAKES

MITCHELL, SD

HOME OF THE CORN PALACE, WHICH IS, UM, A PALACE BUILT OF CORN. THERE ARE GIANT MURALS ALL AROUND THE OUTSIDE MADE FROM 12 DIFFERENT COLORS OF CORN. EVERY SUMMER, THEY TEAR DOWN THE MURALS AND MAKE DIFFERENT ONES. GROWN-UPS...THEY DO THE WEIRDEST THINGS.

HERE I STARTED WONDERING: IF CORN OIL COMES FROM CORN, WHERE DOES BABY OIL COME FROM?

DE SMET, SD

THE LADY WHO WROTE THE LITTLE HOUSE ON THE PRAIRIE BOOKS LIVED HERE WHEN SHE WAS GROWN UP. WE WALKED THROUGH HER HOUSE AND HAD A CHEERFUL PICNIC DINNER IN THE CEMETERY WHERE A BUNCH OF HER FAMILY ARE BURIED. SOOO YEAAAH.

STARTED TO FEEL A LITTLE CARSICK,* SO MOM GAVE ME MEDICINE. FELL ASLEEP AND DREAMED I WAS PRESIDENT. I SIGNED A LAW MAKING IT ILLEGAL TO TAKE AWAY A KID'S ELECTRONICS. YESSS.

ALSO, MY MOM BOUGHT A WEIRD HAT CALLED A BONNET, AND IT'S CREEPING ME OUT!

THIS STATE HAS LAKES LIKE SOME PEOPLE HAVE FRECKLES.

SO LONG, SOUTH DAKOTA.

WALNUT GROVE, MN
WELP, TURNS OUT LAURA INGALLS WILDER LIVED HERE WHEN SHE WAS A <u>KID</u>. (DID SHE LIVE EVERYWHERE?) MOM FOUND OUT A PLAY PERFORMANCE ABOUT LAURA WAS JUST ABOUT TO START IN AN OUTDOOR THEATER. SO GUESS WHAT WE JUST DID. I LEARNED WHAT IT WAS LIKE TO LIVE IN A MUD CAVE AND GET SWARMED BY GRASSHOPPERS. HEARTWARMING STUFF.

(OUR TOUR GUIDE CLAIMED THAT HORSES DON'T EAT KIDS, BUT I'M NOT TAKING ANY CHANCES. THERE'S NO WAY THEY GET THAT BIG EATING GRASS.)

IT'S UBER-LATE, BUT DAD SAYS HE'S GONNA KEEP DRIVING AND WE'LL GO STRAIGHT TO BED WHEN WE GET TO MY COUSINS' HOUSE. I'LL JUST PUT SOME FINISHING TOUCHES ON THIS MAP AND THEN: IT'S ZZZZZZZ TIME...

FAMILY SING-A-LONG! "OLD MACDONALD." SOMEBODY SAVE ME!

THIS IS **IOWA**.
I'VE NEVER BEEN. BUT I LEARNED FROM THE ATLAS THAT IOWA IS ONE OF 10 STATES THAT HAS MORE VOWELS THAN CONSONANTS* IN ITS NAME. THE OTHER 9 ARE...?

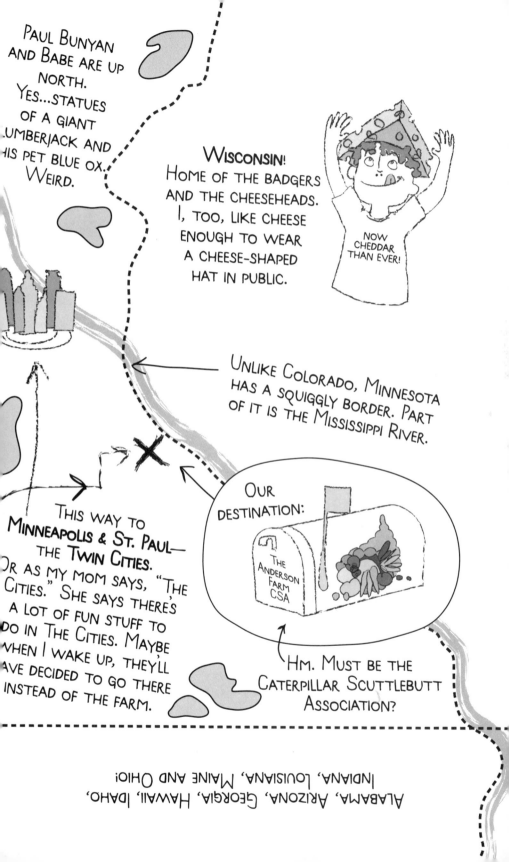

PAUL BUNYAN AND BABE ARE UP NORTH. YES...STATUES OF A GIANT LUMBERJACK AND HIS PET BLUE OX. WEIRD.

WISCONSIN! HOME OF THE BADGERS AND THE CHEESEHEADS. I, TOO, LIKE CHEESE ENOUGH TO WEAR A CHEESE-SHAPED HAT IN PUBLIC.

NOW CHEDDAR THAN EVER!

UNLIKE COLORADO, MINNESOTA HAS A SQUIGGLY BORDER. PART OF IT IS THE MISSISSIPPI RIVER.

OUR DESTINATION:

THE ANDERSON FARM CSA

THIS WAY TO MINNEAPOLIS & ST. PAUL— THE TWIN CITIES. OR AS MY MOM SAYS, "THE CITIES." SHE SAYS THERE'S A LOT OF FUN STUFF TO DO IN THE CITIES. MAYBE WHEN I WAKE UP, THEY'LL HAVE DECIDED TO GO THERE INSTEAD OF THE FARM.

HM. MUST BE THE CATERPILLAR SCUTTLEBUTT ASSOCIATION?

ALABAMA, ARIZONA, GEORGIA, HAWAII, IDAHO, INDIANA, LOUISIANA, MAINE AND OHIO!

WHERE AM I?

Have you ever woken up in a strange place, and for a few scary seconds, you didn't know where you were?

Oh yeah, I finally comprehended.* *The farm.*

It was pretty dark in here, so I dug the headlamp Jack gave me out of my backpack and put it on.

I'm in a tiny little room with a tiny little bed and no windows. I'm pretty sure it's a closet. This must be how Harry Potter felt.

Having wizard powers <u>would</u> be cool, but at least I have toe-spreading skills. I'm uber-flexible, which means I'm awesome at yoga, even though it's not on my list of favorite activities. Yoga is EXERCISE—no matter how much my mom tries to tell me it's not. But toe-wiggling—this feels goood...

Hey, now that I'm waking up, I'm remembering something bizarre that happened last night after I fell asleep in the car. I dreamed of giant carrots. There were two of them. They didn't say anything; they just grinned at me oddly. I told them I knew some people, uh, food they should meet. I also remember hearing a weird noise...like a beep-whine-moan-crash.

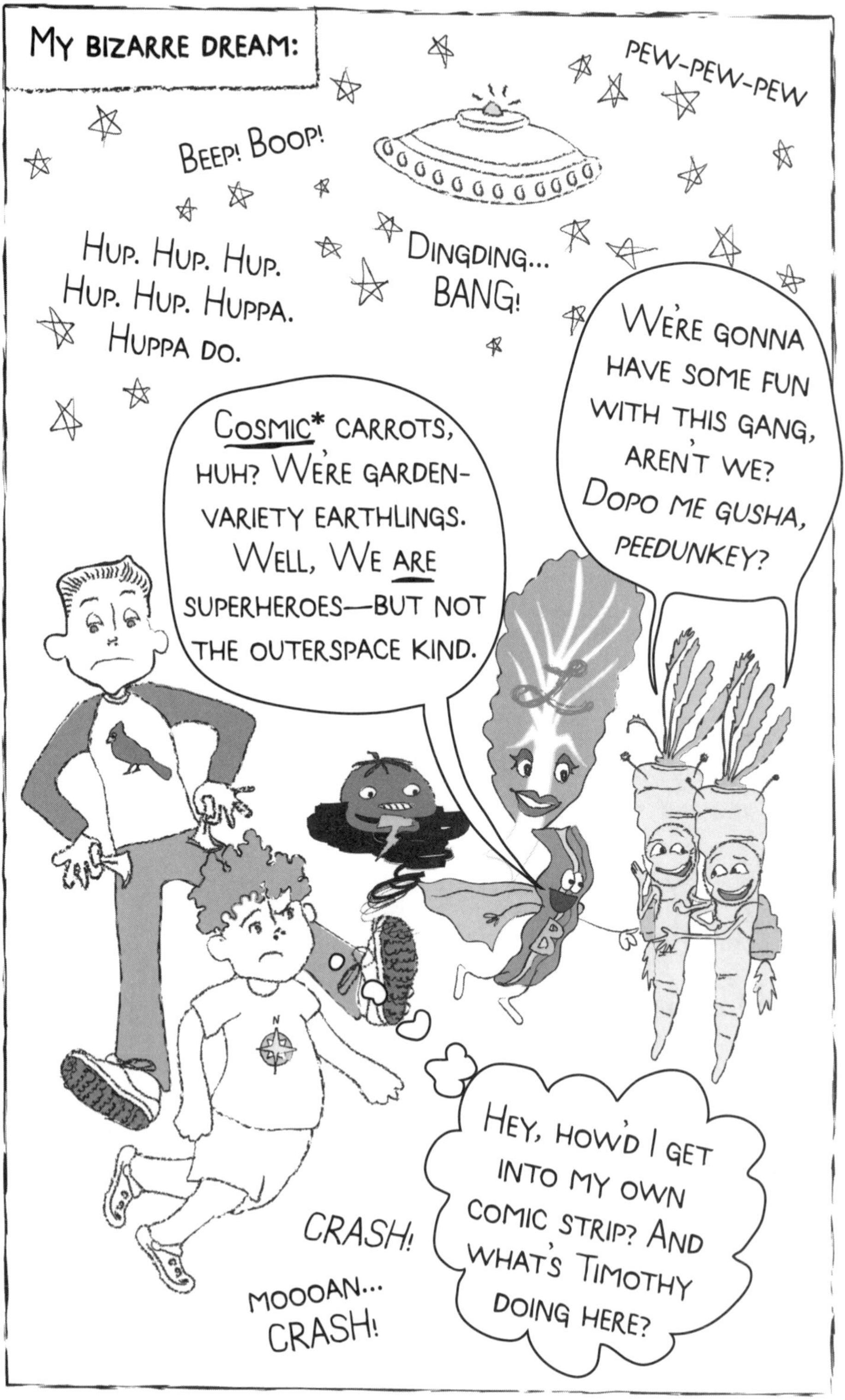

MY BIZARRE DREAM:
PEW-PEW-PEW
BEEP! BOOP!
HUP. HUP. HUP. HUP. HUP. HUPPA. HUPPA DO.
DINGDING... BANG!
WE'RE GONNA HAVE SOME FUN WITH THIS GANG, AREN'T WE? DOPO ME GUSHA, PEEDUNKEY?
COSMIC* CARROTS, HUH? WE'RE GARDEN-VARIETY EARTHLINGS. WELL, WE ARE SUPERHEROES—BUT NOT THE OUTERSPACE KIND.
HEY, HOW'D I GET INTO MY OWN COMIC STRIP? AND WHAT'S TIMOTHY DOING HERE?
CRASH!
MOOOAN... CRASH!

Oh boy, I just smelled my favorite smell. Yup. Bacon! Time to bust out of this closet and go find, in order of immediate importance:

I followed the bacon smell down the hallway to the kitchen, where I found my family, my aunt and uncle, and my cousins all sitting at a long wooden table.

"Good morning, sleepyhead!" said Mom. "Come say hello. You were conked out* when we got here last night, so we put you straight to bed."

She went over and stood on the Anderson side of the table to make introductions.

"Oh hi," I said. "It smells good in here! I'm so hungry I could eat a horse!*"

I sat down and feasted on the deliciousness.
Bacon as thick as 10 Pokémon cards stacked
together. Fluffy scrambled eggs with gooey cheese.
Homemade biscuits coated with homemade butter
and homemade cherry jelly. Milk as thick as cream!

Aunt Caroline ended up giving me a hug and a kiss (embarrassing, but she's nice), and Uncle Odin told knock-knock jokes.

KNOCK-KNOCK!
WHO'S THERE?
INTERRUPTING COW.
INTERRUP...
MOOOOOOOO!

"I think I heard a weird noise last night," I said after I finished eating. "Like whining and a crash."

I caught a clandestine* glance between the twins. Uncle Odin raised an eyebrow at them.

"Oh, uh, you probably heard the ghost," said Chaz-or-Al. (I can't tell them apart.)

"Yeah," said the other twin. "Great-grandfather Aldo. He makes a commotion* at night."

"Oh pshaw," said Uncle Odin. "They're just pulling your leg, aren't you, boys?"

Ghost, schmost. I'm back in my room, letting my food digest. I'm supposed to change into my farm clothes, but I'm in no hurry. It's vacation! I think I'll find the TV now and catch some cartoons.

C U L8R.*

GREEN ACRES

I returned to the kitchen to find someone who could point me in the direction of a TV, but instead I found my mom.

"Oh good, Aldo, I was just about to come looking for you." She was using her chirrupy* voice. "The twins and Timothy are waiting for you out in the chicken coop. Chaz and Al will show you around the farm, and you get to help them with their chores!"

I'M A GROWING BOY. I NEED MY REST!

"Nah," I said. "I'm still tired from our road trip. I'm gonna hang out in here and watch a little TV..." I rubbed my eyes to demonstrate just how much a thousand-mile car ride can take out of a kid.

"There's no TV for you to watch, Aldo," Mom said as if everything was perfectly copacetic.* "Isn't that right, Caroline?"

Aunt Caroline was walking by with a basket of wet laundry. "Correct!"

Well that's as dumb as it gets. At least that's what I was <u>thinking</u>, but I couldn't <u>say</u> it to an aunt I barely knew. "No TV?" I said.

"Nope. No TV," repeated Aunt Caroline. "No newfangled computers, either." She looked at me and winked.

My mouth fell agape.

"Oh you'll be too busy to notice, Aldo," said Mom. "You won't even miss them. Follow me."

I guess I was in shock, because I simply followed my mom out of the house in crestfallen* silence.

(Looking back, I see that I should have thrown a fit at this point. Maybe one of my famous conniptions would have made my mom see the error of her ways.)

Out we marched to this small, red barn
thing with a fenced-in area attached to one side.
Behind the fence, a swarm of chickens strutted
and clucked. Timothy had already gone into the
little chicken jail. Chaz and Al waved at us as we
approached.

"I have the best memories of being on the farm when I was young," Mom whispered to me as she gave me a hug. "Oh, and I know it's hard to tell them apart, but Chaz is the one with the cowlick.*" Then to the twins she said, "Show Timothy and Aldo what farm life is all about! We'll see you at lunchtime." And she left us there together, the city boys and the country boys—like that was perfectly copacetic, too.

"What's wrong with you?" I asked Timothy. As I've mentioned in my other sketchbooks, Timothy is a Super-Jock. He's good at anything athletic. I had expected him to transform into Super-Farmer today, but instead he was looking extremely mopey.

"My iPod is missing. And my cell phone doesn't work here. I can't text!" he said.

He held up the phone screen for me to see. No service.

"Oh. That is weird. But you know what's even weirder? There's no TV here—or computers!" I said.

Meanwhile, Chaz pulled the lid off a big bucket, reached down inside, and scooped up a cupful of little brown pellets. He handed the cup to me. "Who needs TV and computers when you have all this?" he said. He mechanically waved his arm from left to right, including all of the farm's buildings and fields in the sweep of his gesture.

DECLARATION OF INDEPENDENCE
ALL PEOPLE ARE CREATED EQUAL AND HAVE THE RIGHT TO LIFE, LIBERTY, AND THE PURSUIT OF HAPPINESS, WHICH INCLUDES MODERN-DAY ELECTRONICS, FOR CRYING OUT LOUD.

Aldo Timothy

"Yeah," said Al. "Our days are all filled with an easy country charm." He was stooping to pick up an egg on the ground, so I couldn't catch the expression on his face.

Timothy and I gave each other an *Are these guys for real?* look.

48

"This part inside the fence is called 'the run,'" said Chaz, ignoring our questioning expressions. "Aldo, taste the chicken feed first, and if it tastes OK, scatter it around the run."

"Aw c'mon. I'm not eating this," I said, glancing at the funny-looking pellets. "Why do I have to taste it?"

"It's the only way to tell if it's fresh," said Al. "See?" And he popped a pellet into his mouth, chewed it up, and swallowed. "Yep, tastes OK."

I shrugged and sprinkled the chicken food on the ground. The chickens gobbled it up. (Have you ever seen chickens eat? They peck at the ground fast as lightning and snarf anything lying there. Ants, beware!) Finally, there was just one pellet left in the cup, and when no one was looking, I ate it.

NOT BAD. TASTES LIKE CHICKEN.

While I fed the chickens, Timothy and Al went inside the coop to gather eggs. "Ow!" I heard Timothy yell. "Hey! Ow!"

Chaz chuckled. "He must be trying to take Cordelia's eggs. She's broody."

"What does that mean?"

"She likes to sit on her eggs and hatch them. If you try to reach under her to get them, she pecks you."

Oh great, I thought. *No TV and now, killer chickens. In Farm Town, all the animals are <u>nice!</u>*

THOSE COMPUTER CHICKENS ARE SISSIES!

Timothy and Al finally emerged from the coop with a pailful of eggs. Timothy grabbed 3 eggs and began to juggle them. I could tell he was trying to impress our cousins—and he <u>was</u> pretty impressive, I must admit. But Chaz and Al were ignoring him. So he picked up 2 more eggs and began to juggle with <u>5</u>.

"Wow, Timothy, I didn't know you could do that many," I said.

Al was heading out the gate. "Time to milk the cows," he said as he walked away. Then, I swear, he mumbled something that sounded like, "Huppa dee."

"Huppa do," responded Chaz, who watched Timothy for a half a second, then turned to follow Al. Then he called without looking back, "There's chicken poop on your shoe, Timothy!"

So what did my show-off brother do? He stopped concentrating on the eggs and instead looked down at his feet (which, incidentally, were doo-free). And his airborne eggs crashed to the ground... except for one.

Yuck. Yuck! YUCK!

Ew! Doo?! ON MY NEW SHOE?!

"Sorry, bro," Timothy said, handing me a bandana from his pocket.

"Yeah, right!" I said. "Why am I always the one with egg on my face? I hate that you're my brother!"

As I wiped the goop from my head and stormed off after the twins, I passed the clothesline where Aunt Caroline had hung the wet laundry to dry and, next to the clothesline, the farm's gigantic vegetable garden.

Bee was right: The garden did look amazing. *I'll have to draw it for her,* I thought, which made me feel a blip of missingness for Jack and Max and Bogus and everybody back home—where the people are actually nice to me and it's the right century.

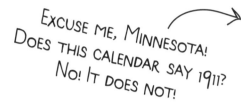

EXCUSE ME, MINNESOTA! DOES THIS CALENDAR SAY 1911? No! IT DOES NOT!

August 2011

I found Chaz and Al in the barn, getting out metal pails, a large sack of something grainy to feed the cows, and a few big buckets. "This here's Larry, Moe, and Curly," said Al. "We have to milk them twice a day. *(Yet another thing to look forward to this week. Oh joy.)*

WHAT HAPPENS IF YOU FORGET TO MILK THEM? DO THEY EXPLODE?

HOW ABOUT WE DON'T FIND OUT.

Chaz sat on a bucket next to Larry. He reached down and squeezed Larry's nozzles, and ta-da! Out sprayed milk into the bucket! It was gross and weird, but also kind of astonishing. Al cozied* up next to Moe, which left me with Curly.

"She's brown," said Al. "So she makes <u>chocolate</u> milk."

He was teasing me—I knew that, duh—but as I wrapped my fingers around Curly's squirter-thingy, I was kinda hoping it was true—and the idea seemed to distract me from the fact that I was actually touching cow nozzles. I squeezed, but nothing came out, white or chocolate.

"It's not working!" I said. My face was right up next to Curly's belly, and I was getting hot and sweaty, which I never enjoy.

"Check to make sure the cap's off!" called Chaz.

So I got real close to the nozzle to see if it was uncapped—and ha-ha, very funny—got sprayed.

"Not cool, Chaz," said Timothy, who must have come in just in time to see what happened.

"Aw, we're just kiddin' around," said Al.

"Yeah," said Chaz. "Don't get your undies in a bunch. It's just milk. Bring Curly's pail into the house when you're done."

"And put away the milking chinnel," they said in unison as they left, each with a bucket of milk and a grin a mile wide.

"What's chinnel?" I asked Timothy through gritted teeth as I wiped my face with the bandana—for the second time in one morning.

"No clue. Hey, do you get the feeling the cuzzes* are ganging up on us?"

"Mostly on me, but yeah."

"We need to stick together then," he said. "You and me...we're going to be a team on this vacation. OK?" And he reached out his hand to shake mine.

WHY DO LEFT-HAN[D] PEOPLE LIKE ME HAV[E] TO SHAKE WITH THEIR RIGHT HANDS? LIFE IS SO UNFAIR.

Me and Timothy, a team? Besides living in the same house and sharing the same Mom and Dad, we don't have much in common. And usually he's not what you'd call <u>considerate</u>* to me.

"Uhhh...OK," I said doubtfully. But I looked in his eyes and shook his hand, and to my surprise I felt a thrilling surge of that team spirit Timothy must feel when he plays sports. I also recognized his competitive* expression; Dad calls it his "game face." And when my brother gets on his game face, you'd better watch out.

I BUTTER NOT TELL YOU

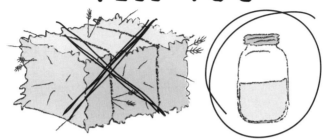

After lunch, Aunt Caroline said it was high time my dad and I learned how to make butter. She made it sound like it was a basic skill all humans should learn: walking, talking, potty-training, tying your own shoes, and making butter.

"Or you can go bale hay with Timothy and your mom and Uncle Odin," she added. "Your choice."

"Hmmm," I said. "How do you bale hay in real life?"

"You're in a big field of cut hay, and you're walking up and down the rows, lifting heavy bales onto the wagon while your uncle runs the tractor," she said. "It's noisy and itchy and hot."

Wow. In Farm Town, you just <u>click</u> to stack hay. "Butter it is!" I decided.

Aunt Caroline had been saving Larry, Moe, and Curly's milk from the past few days in the refrigerator. The thick cream floated near the top of the bottles, and we spooned it off and plopped it into a glass jar until we had about half a jarful.

"Now we screw on the lid and shake the cream," said Aunt Caroline, and she handed me the jar. "Go ahead, Aldo. Shake it up."

So I shook and shook and shook the big, heavy jar. Pretty soon my arms got tired, so I set it down, opened the lid, and looked inside.

"It's not working," I said.

"My turn," Dad said.

So then he shook and shook and shook the big, heavy jar. While he shook it, I watched his cheeks jiggle up and down, and I told him about getting egg on my head and milk in my face. Since Aunt Caroline was in the room and I don't like to be a tattletale, I didn't say that it was the twins' fault that my life was becoming even more miserable than it already was.

But good ol' Dad, he read between the lines. "Where are those rascals, anyway?" he asked Aunt Caroline.

"Good question," she said. "I haven't seen them since lunch. I sent them to pick cauliflower* for dinner, but that only takes a few minutes..."

FOOD THAT LOOKS LIKE A BRAIN. BLECH.

Just then we heard a commotion overhead, and Chaz and Al came clomping* down the back stairs.

"And what have you two been up to?" asked Aunt Caroline.

"Uhhh, we thought we heard the ghost," said Al.

"So we took responsibility for checking it out," said Chaz, and he and Al puffed up their chests identically with fake responsibleness.

Aunt Caroline raised one eyebrow so high it looked like it might disappear into her hair. Then she put her hands on her hips. I knew that mom body language! She didn't believe them.

"There's no ghost," I said.

"Yes there is," said Chaz and Al in unison.

"Then prove it."

"We will."

"Can-n-n I-I-I stop-p-p???" asked my dad. He was still shaking the jar.

Now-w-w IF-F I I-JUST HAD S-S-SOME FR-RIES-S TO G-GO WITH THIS-S SH-H-HAKE...

"Yes, you can stop!" cried Aunt Caroline. "Let's look."

So Dad set the jar down on the kitchen table and let me open it and peer inside. It was full of pale yellow chunks floating in a thin, milky liquid. *Guhross.*

"Nice work, Leo," said Aunt Caroline.

She poured the contents of the jar into a strainer set over a big bowl. The strainer caught the yellow chunks and let the milkiness pass through into the bowl below.

"OK, now we put these chunks into a clean bowl and rinse them with cold water," she said. "Then we mix the chunks together into a single blob, add a sprinkle of salt, and voilà, butter!"

Then Aunt Caroline pulled a loaf of just-baked bread from the oven. She sliced thick hunks and told me and Dad to spread them with the butter we had made. Snack-wise, it was right up there with taquitos.

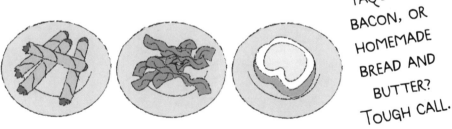

TAQUITOS, BACON, OR HOMEMADE BREAD AND BUTTER? TOUGH CALL.

She also gave me a glass of buttermilk, which was the milky liquid left over from the butter-making. Drink-wise, it was <u>not</u> better than Slushies (my favorite beverage). Not even <u>close.</u>

When Timothy gets back from the hay field, I'm not even gonna brag to him about how much easier and awesomer my chore was than his. Instead, I'm going to tell him about the great idea I just had to score some points for our team. To be safe, I'm not going to write it down, but I <u>will</u> reveal one clue: it involves  = _____.

MISTER ED

Everyone convened* after finishing their hay, cauliflower, and butter chores. Dad put out pitchers of ice water with lemon, and we rested in the shade of the front porch.

"Pssst, Timothy." I beckoned for him to follow me around to the side of the house. When we were safely out of earshot, I whispered, "I have an idea for getting back at the twins. You know how there are two staircases to the upstairs?"

He nodded.

"Welp, I've noticed that the only people who ever use the back stairs are the twins. So here's my plan: let's spread the bottom step with butter—which, by the way, is what I made this afternoon while you were outside slaving away in the hot, noisy hayfield. It was fun. Anyway, they'll slip and fall, and it'll be hilarious."

"Hmm," Timothy said. "I like it."

"Also," I said, "have you noticed that the twins have secret code-words? We need some."

"OK. I'll work on that," said Timothy. "Now let's go butter the step."

We were starting to tiptoe around to the back door when Uncle Odin called, "Boys! It's time to tend the horses. Then you can go for a ride."

I wanted to announce that no way was I getting anywhere near a horse, but Timothy grabbed my arm and pulled me with him.

"We're going horseback riding, bro!" he said, a little too loudly. "Let's do it!"

Let's do it is Timothy-speak for *Our team may be behind, but we can still win this one.*

"Uh, yeah, let's...do it!?" I said.

Mom and Dad looked at me like I'd sprouted a second head. But I ignored them and strode pretend-confidently alongside Timothy in the direction of the barn.

WHAT?! I'VE TOTALLY RIDDEN THE HORSE AT THE GROCERY STORE.

YEAH. RIDING A REAL ONE IS PRACTICALLY THE SAME, RIGHT?

"All you have to know is how to <u>stop</u> a horse," Timothy whispered to me. "In cowboy movies, some dumb guy always climbs on a horse, then some smart guy standing on the ground slaps the horse on the butt, which makes it take off at full-speed. Then the horse runs under a low tree branch and the dumb guy gets clotheslined.*"

"So I'm the dumb guy?" I was frowning with annoyedness, but Timothy wasn't noticing.

"Yes."

"Thanks. So if that happens..."

"So if that happens, just pull back on the reins and say, 'Whoa!' real loud."

"Duh. I'm not 2."

"Good. The other thing to remember is that our team will score points with the adults if we act chipper.* That will also confuse Chaz and Al. We have to play defensively this afternoon, since they have the home-field advantage. Later tonight we'll work on our offense. Got it?"

What Timothy was saying was that we needed to avoid any more egg-on-the-head and milk-in-the-face incidents, pretend to have good attitudes, and tonight, brainstorm more ways to prank the twins.

"Got it."

By now we had reached the barn, and Chaz was grabbing pitchforks and shovels. Al was putting leashes on two colossal horses and walking them outside.

"Let's muck out the stalls while Al saddles up," said Chaz.

One look at the barn floor and I realized what Chaz meant by "muck out." It's basically the same chore as cleaning up dog poop at my house, only here, the pooper is the size of an elephant. So you do the math.

THAT'S IT?

I opened my mouth to argue that I was a guest, and guests never have to worry about pet poop, but Timothy gave me a *Don't you dare* look, so I followed his lead and began shoveling wet straw and uber-chunky poo into the wheelbarrow.

"So have you actually seen this so-called ghost?" I asked Chaz. I glanced up and noticed that Timothy had transformed into Super-Pooper Scooper. He was rapid-firing piles from 10 feet away, and every shot was dead-on.

"Heck yeah," said Chaz. "He wears this old flannel bathrobe, and he clomps his cane across the floor and makes creepy moaning and whining noises. That's when he's <u>inside</u> the house."

"You've seen him outside too?"

"Sure. Sometimes he's in the forest over there." He pointed. "My dad said that when Old Aldo was alive, he liked to walk in those woods."

Oh c'mon. He's just trying to get to me, even though his voice sounds like he's telling the truth... He's probably just a good liar. Who cares. I ain't afraid of no ghost. So, instead of giving him the satisfaction of asking more ghost questions, I whistled a happy tune. (That's what you do when you want people to think you're perfectly at ease.)

Soon the mucking was done, and Chaz and Timothy were pitchforking fresh, clean hay around the stall. It looked sorta cozy.

Then Chaz told us to follow him outside the barn, where Al and the horses were waiting.

"This here's Starlight," said Al. "Timothy, you'll ride him. And Aldo, you can take Mr. Ed. Have you two ridden before?"

"Sure," lied Timothy. "A bunch of times. What are you guys gonna do?"

"Oh, we'll walk alongside," said Chaz. "Make sure you're havin' fun."

The parents waved to us from the front porch.

"OK, Aldo, Mr. Ed's all ready. Go ahead and mount," said Al.

This is a game, just like Farm Town, I reminded myself. *Timothy's on my team. I can do this.* So I pasted a smile onto my face and walked over to Mr. Ed. He watched me with his huge brown-marble eye, but at least he didn't try to eat me. He just stood there like a living, breathing mountain. I tried to stick my foot into the foot-holder thingy dangling from the saddle, but I couldn't reach it. It was too high.

Luckily Timothy saw the problem before I even said anything. He came to my side, laced the fingers of his hands together, and told me to put my left foot into his palms. Then he hoisted me up.

"Hold the reins," Timothy whispered. "Sit up straight and act like you know what you're doing."

Mr. Ed must be the tallest and widest horse that ever lived. I was at least 20 feet up in the air, and my legs were so far apart I was practically doing the splits.

Timothy swung easily up onto Starlight. He picked up the reins and made a clicking noise with the side of his mouth. He totally looked like he knew what he was doing! (I guess that's the advantage of being athletic. And watching old movies.)

Starlight started to walk, and Mr. Ed followed! I didn't even have to click. Timothy was steering us to the woods at the edge of the field.

"Uh, Timothy, those woods..." I said. "Chaz said there's something out there..."

But Timothy didn't seem to hear me, and I didn't want the twins to catch me yelling about ghosts. So we kept heading toward the trees, and my heart started doing backflips.

As soon as we were in the woods, where the parents couldn't see us, I saw Al tap Starlight on the butt and say, "Ha!"

Starlight took off, and I could feel Mr. Ed gathering himself beneath me to take off too.

But Timothy, who is too good a contender to be distracted by ghost stories, was prepared. He pulled back on the reins immediately and bellowed, "Whoa!" Starlight stopped. Mr. Ed stopped.

"We're on to you guys," said Timothy. "You two are in cahoots* against us. But watch out, cuz now we're in cahoots right back at ya."

Chaz and Al's four eyes went wide with surprise.

"Jeeby," said Al.
"Jeeby-jo," said Chaz.

"What???" I said, but Timothy had already clicked and was steering us back in the direction of the house, toward the grown-ups.

Considering horses are <u>probably</u> the scariest mammals ever to walk the earth, I'd been doing OK so far. But then Timothy clicked again, and Starlight began to jog! And guess what Mr. Ed-the-copycat* did. My whole body bounced up-and-down, side-to-side, up-and-down as he ran.

I started to feel carsick. I took a quick peek back and saw that the twins were way behind us. "Let's slow down!" I called to Timothy.

Unfortunately, my brother's favorite speed is hyper-speed. Starlight kept running. I tried tugging on Mr. Ed's leash and telling him to whoa, but he ignored my authority.

We raced up to the porch, where Timothy performed a showy sideways halt. Mr. Ed stopped, too, though not as elegantly. My mom was holding her camera, and just as I saw her raise it to her face to take our picture, I leaned over Mr. Ed's side and chucked up all that homemade bread and butter.

What a waste.

HERE'S HOW THAT GREAT PHOTO MY MOM TOOK
TURNED OUT.

LUCKY FOR THEM, NO HORSES GOT PUKED
ON—ONLY THE GROUND. HEY, I JUST NOTICED
THAT STARLIGHT AND MR. ED SEEM TO BE
COMMUNICATING WITH EACH OTHER. THEY'RE
MIND-READING HORSES! MAYBE THEY'RE IN
CAHOOTS WITH THE GHOST TOO...

WHITTLE ME THIS

By dinnertime I had recovered enough to nibble
on the delicious porkchops Aunt Caroline served.
Afterward, Uncle Odin said it was high time
Timothy and I learned how to whittle. *Oh great.*
Walking, talking, potty-training, tying your own
shoes, making butter, and now, whittling.

So we all sat on the front porch—again.
Uncle Odin found some scraps of wood and pocket-
knives, and we kids tried our hand at whittling
while the others sewed with some silly wooden
circles.

"What do you
miss most about the
farm, Claire?" asked
Uncle Odin.

My mom got a
faraway look in her eyes. "I miss when we all
lived here together—me, you, Mom and Dad,
Grandfather Aldo. Remember how simple life was
then?"

Uncle Odin sighed. "Sure 'nough do."

"I love Colorado," said my mom. "But you're lucky to still have the farm."

"Yes, life on the farm is kinda laid back," agreed Aunt Caroline.

"Just look how rosy Aldo's cheeks have already gotten!" Mom said. And she leaned over and grabbed my face. For Timothy's sake, I played along and smiled up at her.

While the grown-ups were reminiscing and the twins were caught up in their whittling, Timothy and I tiptoed into the house, scooped some butter in our hands, and spread it all over the bottom step of the back staircase.

Then we went back outside to join the others.

Uncle Odin had brought out a violin (except he called it a fiddle). He could <u>kinda</u> play a few songs, like "Mary Had a Little Lamb" and "Twinkle, Twinkle," but they sounded awfully screechy and terrible, if you ask me.

Pretty soon it got dark, and a bunch of itty-bitty flashing lights appeared in the field.

"Oh look, Aldo, fireflies!" said Mom.

Dad went inside and brought out a couple of jars with screw-on lids for catching the flying bugs, which actually have <u>blinking bulbs</u> <u>stuck to their butts</u>. How cool is that?

Timothy and I competed with the twins to see who could catch the most. We won. *Take that, Chaz and Al.*

(Unfortunately, a herd of mosquitoes also showed up, and now I'm covered with mosquito bites. Before I went to bed, Aunt Caroline dabbed this wet pink stuff called calamine lotion* on the bites so they don't itch. Weird.)

Timothy let me bring the firefly jar into my little room so I could set it on the table next to my bed. I'm watching them blink while I write this. Next to the jar, in the glow of the firefly light, I placed my whittling project.

Oh, and I thought I had stepped in some mud piles as I walked around the farm today. Turns out they weren't <u>mud</u> piles. Now that I'm a horse poop expert and I'm sitting here in bed, I can see that the clods* of brown stuff stuck to the bottom of my shoes don't really look—or smell—like mud. So yeaaahhh... Good thing I'm a mouth-breather.

A BAD NIGHT'S SLEEP

Whoa. This place is downright creepy in the middle of the night.

Some weird noise just woke me up, and until I flicked on my headlamp, it was so dark I couldn't even see my fingers in front of my face! I could smell them, though. They smell like those yummy porkchops we had for dinner. What I like to do is dip my chop into my potatoes and get a little of both in each bite...

WHO NEEDS BARBECUE SAUCE WHEN YOU CAN DUNK YOUR MEAT IN THE ULTIMATE CONDIMENT:* MASHED POTATOES!

Hey, there's that high-pitched moaning again. It sounds like a cat caterwauling* in a closet full of lint balls. Uhhh... I'm gonna go find Dad and uhhh... make sure he's OK.

So, I sprinted up the back stairs to the room where Mom and Dad were sleeping. But as soon as my bare foot touched the bottom step, I realized my mistake. _The butter!_ Up flew the bottom half of my body and down crashed the top half. It hurt. A lot. But I picked myself up and kept running until I reached the upstairs hall, where I then slipped on a random carpet and went flying down the shiny wood floor smack into a door at the end of the hallway.

I lay there stunned for a minute, waiting for somebody to come running and call 911. But nobody came! I got the wind knocked out of me, so I couldn't even groan properly. What does it take to get some sympathy around here? Sheesh.

Finally I rolled over onto my side, and my headlamp shone up onto the little door. And on the door hung an old photo of an old man. It was one of those black-and-white photographs that are so ancient they're brownish-yellow. The old guy was scowling at me, so I scowled back at him.

That's when it happened. He winked. I swear, the codger* winked at me! I scrambled to my feet and careened* back down the hallway into my parents' room. I slammed the door behind me and catapulted* into bed between them.

"This stupid farm is haunted!" I yelled.

"It's just old and creaky, Aldo," whispered Mom. "Go back to sleep." And she reached over and clicked off my headlamp.

"Didn't you <u>hear</u> me out there? I was practically dying. In fact, I'm probably <u>still</u> going to die from my injuries in the next two minutes."

"You're fine. Close your eyes."

"As soon as the sun comes up, I'm stealing our car and driving myself home."

"Shhh," said Dad.

"If you could see my face, you would see how mad I am at you for making me come here."

TIMOTHY, JUMP IN! LET'S GET OUTTA HERE!

"I know," said Mom. "Goodnight."

Then she rubbed my back in that irresistible way that calms me down even when I'm sure I'll never be calm again. And I must have fallen asleep, because now it's early morning. I came back downstairs to get my sketchbook and brought it into the bathroom with me. That's where I'm sitting right now.

Gaa, what's that awful noise I hear <u>this</u> time?

THE CRACK OF DAWN

I looked out the bathroom window and spotted the source of the cacophony.* It was the farm's rooster, Chanticleer. My windowless bedroom must have protected me from his earsplitting cock-a-doodle-doo the first morning we were here. Myth: Farms are peaceful and relaxing...and clickable. Reality: Farms are noisy and stinky and tiring.

EVERYBODY UP! THERE'S NO SNOOZE BUTTON ON TALENT LIKE MINE.

I went to breakfast, which was disappointingly unfeastlike today. Just oatmeal and fruit. No pork in sight. Not even <u>Canadian</u> bacon* (which, as everyone knows, is <u>bogus</u> bacon).

"I'm so tired," I said to anyone who would listen. "That creepy noise woke me up again in the middle of the night. When I went upstairs to, you know, check it out, some old dude on the wall winked at me."

Chaz and Al yawned. Come to think of it, they looked really tired too. So did Timothy. But then he always looks zombified before noon.

"That's Old Aldo," said Chaz, stretching. "Maybe he's trying to communicate with you."

"Yeah," said Al. "You might wanna steer clear of his picture...unless you have a hankerin' to meet a dead guy. That portrait is a portal for his ghost."

"You boys are full of baloney this morning," said Mom. "Aldo and Timothy, come gather eggs with me, and I'll tell you about your great-grandfather."

I wish I was full of baloney this morning, I thought.

We slipped on our shoes and stepped outside. "Aldo was your great-grandfather, which means he was my grandfather," Mom continued as we walked to the chicken coop. "So I knew him. In fact, when I was growing up, he lived here with us in the farmhouse. His room was in the attic."

"We should go check out that attic, Aldo," said Timothy.

"I think not," I said. "That guy is creepy." We were inside the chicken run now. I scooped feed from the bucket and tested a piece while I scattered it for the chickens swarming around my feet.

"He wasn't creepy," said Mom. "But he was a prankster."

"What kind of pranks?" I asked.

"Oh, he'd put salt in the sugar bowl. He'd reset the clocks to make Odin and me think we were late for school. Once he set a paper sack full of chicken feathers on top of a door that was ajar, so when I pushed the door open, the feathers dumped onto my head. Things like that."

"Cool," said Timothy. He raised his eyebrows at me with a *Those are good ideas, so remember them* look.

"He also liked to sing and play the fiddle, especially a pretty old song about an Indian maiden." Mom began to sing it for us.

"Watch out for her!" Timothy interrupted, pointing to Cordelia. "She tried to bite my hand off yesterday."

"Yeah, she's broody," I added.

"She's feeling motherly," Mom said.

Yup, I thought. *Sounds about right.*

JUST GIVE ME A SIGN

Timothy taught me these hand-signals today. Just like in baseball. We'll use them against the twins' secret code and out-prank them.

UNSCREW THE CAP TO THE SALT SHAKER AND PASS THE SALT TO CHAZ OR AL.

HEAD ON OVER TO THE BARN. HIDE IN THE HAY, THEN JUMP OUT AND SPIT WATERMELON SEEDS AT CHAZ AND AL WHEN THEY'RE MILKING THE COWS.

TUCK A LITTLE COW PRESENT UNDER THE TWINS' PILLOWS.

PUT SHOE POLISH ON THE RIMS OF MOM'S BINOCULARS. HAND THE BINOCULARS TO CHAZ AND AL AND TELL THEM THE SKY IS FALLING OR SOMETHING.

MEET AT THE DOOR TO THE ATTIC AND CONFRONT* THE GHOST.

TIME TO GO FISHING. WHAT?!

CHEETAHS NEVER WIN

Before dinner, Aunt Caroline sent Timothy, the twins, and me out to pick cucumbers. She gave us each a basket and an old pair of scissors and told us not to come back to the house until our baskets were full to the tippy-top.

Thinking this was a chance to show up the twins, Timothy made me sprint out to the garden with him. I reminded him that it's <u>never</u> a good idea to run with scissors, but he was less concerned with my safety than he was with victory.

Did you know that cucumbers are prickly? They hurt when you grab them! *Welp, yet another deadly farm task.* I learned to snip the stem with the scissors and let the cucumber fall into the basket without touching it.

When our baskets were almost full, I heard a funny noise coming from behind the tall rows of corn. It sounded high-pitched and screechy. I looked around and saw one of the twins lounging in the shade of a nearby tree. The other one was nowhere in sight.

"Timothy, what's that sound?" I whispered.

"Who cares. Finish picking, Aldo. They're not even trying. We can win this one."

"It's creepy."

"Focus, Zelnick!"

Just then a figure in flowing white came rushing down the garden row toward us. I must admit, I lost my cool. I might even have screamed a tiny bit, and when I dove next to Timothy, I knocked him over and landed on top of him.

The figure sped by, and I saw his familiar-looking shoes. He grabbed my basket in one hand and Timothy's in the other.

"Get off me, Aldo!" said Timothy.

"It was Chaz-or-Al! His cowlick-area was covered up with a white sheet! But it doesn't matter—he carried off our cucumbers!"

I rolled to the side, and Timothy was up and running before you could say Peter Piper.

Now, I know I've pointed out that Timothy is a Super-Jock, but I'm not sure I've ever made it clear how fast he is. Let's put it this way: If Timothy were four-legged, he'd be an uber-cheetah.

HEY DUDE, I'M THE FASTEST LAND MAMMAL.

NOPE. YOU ONLY RUN TO SURVIVE. I RUN FOR A MORE COMPELLING* REASON: TO WIN!

I didn't see what happened next because they were so far ahead of me, but Timothy ended up presenting the cucumbers to Aunt Caroline. She thanked him and scolded the twins, then she sent them to bring in the rest of the dry laundry from the clothesline. (That's where Al got the sheet for his little ghost-in-the-garden charade.*)

Score one for the Brothers Zelnick.

And now I get to chillax in my room while the twins do chores. Whew!

Oh, and a letter came today from Mr. Mot. I miss the old guy. And I really miss Maxie—the cutest, smartest, bestest dog in the world.

Hm. Speaking of pets, I'm noticing that the fireflies in the jar next to my bed aren't looking so chipper. I think I'll step outside and let them go.

Life—it's a roller-coaster of carefree* butt-blinking followed by being trapped into doing things you don't want to do, getting bounced around till you're carsick, and hopefully, if you're lucky, getting back to where you belong.

Hello, Aldo!

What a wonderful week Max and I are having! I am thoroughly enjoying his canine companionship.* Thrice daily we walk to the capacious* dog park. Max is quite a charismatic* presence there and has already made many new friends.

This afternoon we baked homemade doggie cookies, chock-full* of pureed carrots, garlic, rolled oats, and wheat germ. Max must not want to spoil his dinner, for he has politely refused them thus far.

What a wonderful time you must be having with the Andersons. Perhaps you are playing canasta* for entertainment of an evening?

Cordially,*

Mr. Mot

MOOVE!

After dinner tonight (chicken and dumplings—yumbo), we all played horseshoes. The Zelnicks beat the Andersons. Timothy whooped and high-fived me and led our family in a little victory dance.

WHOA! THESE BABIES ARE HEAVY!

Then, when we'd finished celebrating, he suddenly got all serious-faced and gave me the meet-me-at-the-attic sign.

LIGHTWEIGHT, COMFY, AND DOESN'T HAVE TO BE NAILED TO YOUR FOOT

Mom, in her momness, noticed him scratching his head. "I think you need a shower, Timothy," she said.

"Uh...OK, I'll head upstairs and take a shower," he said loudly, exaggerating the monkey-scratch motion and looking directly at me.

I played it cool with the fam for a minute or two after Timothy went inside, then I followed him. Sure enough, I found him upstairs, his eye to the keyhole in the attic door.

"It's locked," he said. "But I bet I can open it. I practiced lock-picking when I was learning those magic tricks this summer. I just need a paper clip."

"I don't think they have paper clips on farms." It was getting dark, and Old Aldo, hanging in his frame on the door, was looking exceptionally cantankerous.*

Just then Chaz and Al came running down the hallway toward us.

"Hey, what're you two up to?" Al asked breathlessly.

"We decided we should introduce ourselves to your ghost," said Timothy.

"Old Aldo doesn't take kindly to strangers," said Chaz.

"We're not strangers—we're family," said Timothy.

"Well, I'm a stranger," I mumbled. "Just because we have the same name doesn't mean we should ever, like, come anywhere near each other..."

"Hey, I just thought of something more fun we could do after the parents go to bed," said Al, putting his arms around Timothy's and my shoulders and leading us back down the hallway. "Let's go cow-tipping."

"Cool," said Timothy, who's always up for a new sport—and who expects his team members to be equally enthusiastic.

"Cool," I lied.

We went to our bedrooms and pretended to go to sleep. I lay there, worrying. *How do you tip a cow? Why do you tip a cow? Is it really necessary for a person to tip a cow, like making butter and whittling?*

But eventually Chaz and Al and Timothy came and got me, and we snuck outside. The night was warm, and the full moon lit the farm like a celestial* headlamp.

"We're gonna head over to the Fitschens' pasture," whispered Al. "It's right there, on the other side of our fence."

"Shhh," said Chaz. "If we wake up the cows, it won't work."

As we picked our way across the field, I started to get <u>really</u> apprehensive. Cows may not be quite as gigantic as horses, but they're plenty big and scary, especially in the dark.

Soon we came upon a clump of cows. They were standing like statues in the moonlight. "See that one off by herself?" whispered Chaz.

"Yeah," Timothy answered.

"She's a good one. You and Aldo just need to get a running start then <u>push</u>. She'll topple right over."

I pictured the cow falling on her side with a thud. "I don't get it," I said.

"It's just funny," said Al. "And the cow doesn't get hurt."

"<u>You</u> go tip it then," I said.

"Aw, we tip them all the time," said Chaz. "We're out here so <u>you two</u> can experience it."

"C'mon, Aldo," said Timothy. "I've heard guys talk about cow-tipping. It'll be <u>awesome</u>. Let's do it."

Uh-oh. There was that "*We can still win*" phrase again.

So in support of my team, I, Aldo Valentine Zelnick, snuck up on a dozing cow in a cowpie-dotted field in the middle of nowhere in the middle of the night. Timothy silently signaled 1, 2, 3! with his fingers, and when he got to 3, we ran at the cow.

THANKS FOR THE GREAT MIDDLE NAME, MOM AND DAD.

And she trotted away.

"Welp, that was awfully entertaining," I said. "We'd better get to bed." I stretched and covered my fake yawn with my hand. "I'm sure we have a big day of farm fun ahead of us tomorrrrow."

"Try again," said Al. "There. That one." He pointed to a shortish cow at the edge of the clump.

"C'mon, Aldo. One more time," said Timothy, who is fearless when it comes to, well, everything.

"All right," I muttered.

So Timothy counted to 3 again, and we ran at the midget cow, and guess what. It wasn't a midget cow. It was a calf.* And it turns out mom cows are just like mom chickens and mom humans. They're cranky.* In fact, the whole clump of cows began to run at us now.

Timothy and I turned to escape and saw that the twins had already taken off.

"Run, Aldo!" yelled Timothy.

"I am running!"

Remember how I said that Timothy is beat-a-cheetah fast? Well, I'm not. In fact, I'm the slowest runner in my school. And now the killer cows were gaining on me!

"You go ahead!" I called to Timothy. "Save yourself!"

But Timothy, welp, he's my brother. He had my back. He turned around and ran past me, at the cows, yelling like a crazy man.

Timothy scared the cows away. Me, I stumbled and fell, which you never want to do in a cow field, trust me. But Timothy came and helped me up, and as we walked back to the farmhouse together, he kept hopping back and forth and punching the air.

"Good job out there tonight, bro," he said.

"You too."

"Yeah, we showed those cows who's boss."

"We didn't tip any, though."

"No biggie. I bet the twins have never tipped one either."

Then Timothy looked at me and plugged his nose.

"You're gonna cow-pie their pillows...right now?" I asked.

"Yup." And he took the bandana out of his pocket and used it to grab the cow doo that was, apparently, stuck to my pant leg.

"I'll take care of this," he said with a wink. "You go get some shut-eye, pardner."

Brothers. Most of the time it seems like you'd be better off without them, but every once in a while they prove you wrong.

P.S.
No COWS WERE HARMED IN THE MAKING OF THIS CHAPTER.

IT WAS A HOOT

For breakfast today, there were warm, crispy stacks of bacon again and cooked eggs in cool little cups. They're just toying with me here. Bacon! *No bacon.* Bacon! *No bacon.*

When Chaz and Al came to the table (freshly showered... Did their hair get dirty in the night, perhaps?), Timothy gave me the "unscrew the salt cap" sign. So I loosened the lid then casually set the salt shaker on the table near Al.

Al was loading his plate with an egg and some bacon when Aunt Caroline looked up from the book she was reading, reached across the table for the shaker, and before I could warn her, dumped an avalanche of salt on top of her egg.

"I see you boys have embraced the spirit of Great-grandfather Aldo," was all she said.

After breakfast, I helped Aunt Caroline make dill pickles from all those cucumbers we collected yesterday. Pickles come from cucumbers! And "dill" isn't a kind of flavoring—it's a plant! Who knew?

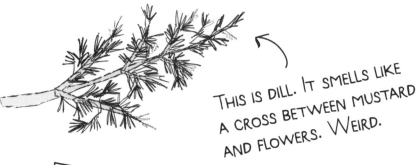

THIS IS DILL. IT SMELLS LIKE A CROSS BETWEEN MUSTARD AND FLOWERS. WEIRD.

GRANDMA GINNY'S DILL PICKLES

- CUCUMBERS
- ONIONS
- VINEGAR
- SUGAR (LOTS)
- SALT
- DILL

CUT THE CUCUMBERS INTO PICKLE-LOOKING STRIPS AND PLOP THEM INTO BIG JARS. THROW SOME ONION AND DILL INTO THE JARS TOO. COOK THE VINEGAR, SUGAR, AND SALT TOGETHER UNTIL THE SUGAR MELTS, ADD WATER, THEN POUR THIS SWEET-SOUR LIQUID OVER THE STUFF IN THE JARS. PICKLES! (DON'T EAT THEM RIGHT AWAY, THOUGH. THEY HAVE TO SOAK IN THE SAUCE FOR A WHILE.)

Later, Uncle Odin marched us all out to the farm's orchard to pick apples. Just beyond the orchard, on the neighbor's farm, some sheep were chillaxing in a field.

"Oh look at the ewes!" Mom said.

"The me's?"

"The you's."

"That's what I said."

"No, Aldo, the e-w-e-s," spelled Mom. "That's what a female sheep is called—a ewe."

Why grown-ups think they have to fill kids' brains with useless information, I'll never understand. Sigh.

WHAT DO YOU GET IF YOUR SHEEP STUDIES KARATE?

A LAMB CHOP!

As we were walking back to the house with our basketful of apples, we heard an "ooooooo" noise coming from the woods!

"It's Old Aldo," said Chaz.

"Let's go check it out," said Timothy, grabbing me by the back of my shirt in a brotherly way and yanking me toward the trees.

"Nah, I'm gonna go help Dad bake apple pies...," I said.

"Oh Aldo, it's a wonderful forest!" gushed Mom. "Odin and I played there all the time when we were kids. And yes, Great-grandfather Aldo loved it too. Come on. I'll show you."

So we stalked courageously* into the deep, dark woods, which is where scary things <u>always</u> happen. *Hansel and Gretel. Little Red Riding Hood. Where the Wild Things Are.* Need I say more?

Mom led us down a path that twisted and turned. Twigs cracked underfoot. Leaves rustled. Then we heard it again, closer this time. "Oooooo...."

"This way," beckoned Mom. "I want to see if the bench Great-grandfather Aldo made is still there."

We came to a clearing. Sure enough, there sat an old wooden bench, rotting in the shadowy wetness of the forest floor. And what was that hanging in thin air next to the bench? It was...a bathrobe...holding a cane!

"Aaahh!" I said. "It's like that story about the pale green pants with nobody inside them!"

"Shhh," whispered Mom. She lifted her binoculars to her eyes and looked. "I see him."

"You do???" said Chaz and Al, who by this point were looking kinda green themselves.

"Yes! It's a gorgeous screech owl."

Whew.

She handed her binoculars to the twins, who each took a turn. Then they passed them to Timothy. He wiped them on his shirt before looking. After Timothy was done, it was my chance to see the screechy little knucklehead.

SCREECHY?!
WHOOO, ME?

Eventually Mom picked up the bathrobe and the cane, which the twins admitted they'd hung there as a joke, and we all returned to the house. I'm here resting in my closet thinking about the day. I sure hope no one comes to get me and tells me it's time to make balloons from pigs' bladders or something.

I also hope Mom doesn't notice the black circles. Timothy shoe-polished the binoculars' rims earlier today to prank the twins, but then Mom grabbed the binoculars to take out to the apple orchard...

I'M NOTICING.

(Sorry 'bout that, Mom!)

Oh, and letters came from Jack and Bee today. It's kinda weird that they both sent me mail...maybe they just miss me. I wish I could meet them at our fort right now. I'd play Crazy Eights with them until the cows come home.*

Hi Aldo.

Bogus is good. The fort is good. Bee is good.

I called your house today to say Hey, let's go get a Slushie, but you didn't answer. That's when I remembered I was supposed to check on Bogus. As I said, he's cool.

So, qué tal? How's life with no video games? That's dumb, huh.

Hasta luego.

Jack

TO: Aldo Zelnick
The Anderson Farm
Goodhue, Minnesota
55027

Hey, how does Jack know about the no-video-game situation? Something fishy (besides Bogus) is going on here.

Dear Aldo, 👁 have been 🧹 +PING for a ✉ from you but nothing has arrived yet. 👁 🐝 + 🍃 that you'll have 👔 +M for this week! 🪝 🐑 +ING what GR+8 adventures R 🐑 having? 🤌 +OULD M+ 🧹 -R me a 🗺 of their 💂 +EN. that school starts 🪝 soon? Your 🏫 -ACE, 🧚 p.s. ✳ and 👁 +X/y +ED something new to the 4+T. It's a surprise!

SQUARE-DANCING

After dinner tonight, we were getting ready to go to a dance (eye roll), when guess who came roaring up on her motorcycle. Goosy!!!

She LOVED the idea of dancing, of course, so she climbed into our car, and we all drove to the town hall.

"I rode through the Black Hills of South Dakota and displayed one of my paintings in a motorcycle art show," she said. "What have you been up to, Aldo?"

"Nothing. It's boring here."

"I've missed you and your curmudgeonly* self!" she said, and she sloppy-kissed me on both cheeks.

"There are no TVs or computers. And I have to do chores. Hard chores!"

"And now you get to go dancing!"

"Exactly!"

Inside the town hall, fiddle music was playing (only this fiddle music actually sounded like music). And there was a refreshments table loaded with homemade cookies—peanut butter, chocolate chip, snickerdoodles (not as good as my dad's, but still tasty), lemon bars, and lots more.

Have you noticed that it's easier to feel happy when you have unlimited access to copious* amounts of cookies? I was just sampling my third lemon bar when Mom dragged me onto the dance floor.

"They're getting the square-dancing started," said Mom. "You and I will be partners; Aunt Caroline will be with Chaz, Odin with Al, and Goosy with Timothy. Just follow my lead."

Square-dancing involves standing in a circle (hellooo!) with the 7 other people in your group. The fiddle player starts to play, and a guy with a microphone jabbers constantly and tells you what to do. Basically, it's his job to confuse you.

At first he gives an easy command, like "Circle to the left," which is where you all hold hands and walk in a clockwise* circle. No problemo. But then he starts saying crazy stuff like "doe-see-doe" and "allumond" and "promunodd," and you're hooking arms and spinning and criss-crossing cattywampus* with someone on the opposite side of your circle until you get to feeling so sweaty and carsick that you have to sit down and have another cookie.

Timothy brought me a lemonade and sat beside me. He handed me his bandana, which I used to mop up my sweaty forehead.

116

Then I sucked my mouth into fish lips.
"The ghost in the woods might've turned out
to be bogus," I said, "but I think you're right:
there's something fishy going on upstairs in the
farmhouse."

"True dat."

"Can you get us into the attic tonight after
everyone goes to bed?"

"Yup. The cock crows at midnight."

"No he doesn't. Chanticleer crows at like 6 in
the morning."

"Bro, it's a code phrase that means we'll
meet at the attic door at midnight."

I knew that.

WHO YA GONNA CALL?

By the time I got to the attic door, Timothy was already on his knees, picking the lock. We could hear moaning and thumping noises behind the door. Old Aldo glared at me, then he blinked!

"Timothy! He's alive!"

But Timothy didn't flinch. He jumped to his feet and swung the door wide open. And what was mounted to the back of the door, behind Old Aldo's portrait? Some kind of fancy video camera!

"Well, well, well...," said Timothy.

A steep, narrow staircase rose in front of us. It was pitch dark, but luckily I'd worn my headlamp. Now we could hear the shrieky, moany, beepy noises even better. They were coming from the top of the stairs.

"You go first," whispered Timothy. "You've got the light."

"I'm not really a 'go first' kinda guy..."

"Tonight's the night you become one."

Has someone ever said something to you that made you change your mind just a little, in a good way, about who you are and what you're capable* of? Yeah. That didn't happen this time. I made Timothy go first.

We tiptoed up the stairs. They creaked, but the attic cacophony drowned out the creakiness. As we rose, I began to see that the attic glowed. What the heck? Was it aliens instead of a ghost? I'd heard of crop circles*... My heart jackhammered in my chest.

At the very top of the staircase, my fingers felt a light switch, and I flipped it up. Suddenly the whole attic was illuminated, and what Timothy and I saw made my mouth drop open and my knees buckle.

(THIS IS WHAT'S KNOWN AS A "CLIFFHANGER.*")

It was like walking into Willy Wonka's chocolate factory: a place of perfection beyond your awesomest dreams.

"Uh...hi!" said Chaz.

"Yeaaahhhh...We're not supposed to be up here...," said Al. "So at least for tonight, let's keep it cool, OK?"

"Would you like to join us?" said Chaz. "You're our guests, so please pick any device and game you want."

Timothy and I said nothing. We were like people dying of thirst who,

unexpectedly and against all odds, had stumbled into an oasis.

We didn't ask questions. Instead, we simply drank it all in.

I picked up a GameBoy, sank to my knees, and began to play. Timothy pulled his cell phone from his pocket and discovered it worked here, in this electronic sanctuary of bliss. He sprawled on the floor and started texting, his fingers clumsy from lack of use.

On we played into the night, hopping from one machine to the next: jamming to tunes on iPods, laughing at videos on

YouTube, battling 2-on-2 on *Mario Smash Brothers* and finally falling asleep to reruns of some ancient TV show about a guy named Wilbur whose horse could talk. (The horse said he doesn't play horseshoes because his mom taught him not to throw his clothes around. Moms. Sheesh!)

When Chanticleer woke me up, I stood and stretched. Timothy and the twins were sprawled on the attic floor in a tangled heap of cords and controllers. I went back to my bedroom to spend some time with this sketchbook. It helps me collect my thoughts.

Actually, now that I'm collecting them, I don't know what to think about everything that's happened this week. To tell the truth, I'm starting to feel annoyed. After all, nobody likes being a butt—especially the butt of a joke.

BREAKFAST OF CHUMPS*

Welp, now I've seen, up close and personal, how the people who supposedly love you the most can gang up on you like a vicious swarm of mosquitoes.

When I walked into the kitchen for breakfast, all the usual people were there, yet everything was different. Aunt Caroline's hair and clothes had changed. Actually, the entire Anderson family looked weirdly contemporary.* Uncle Odin was reading the morning newspaper on an iPad. Chaz and Al were lost in their machines. A flat-panel TV blared cartoons.

"Good morning, Aldo!" said Mom. "We understand you and Timothy made a discovery in the attic last night. Surpri-i-ise!"

"It was your mom's idea to collaborate* with your aunt and uncle and cousins to give you boys an old-fashioned vacation," said Dad. "Pretty nifty, huh?"

"You were all in cahoots against me and Timothy?" I said, appalled. I looked at Timothy, and he shrugged his shoulders as if to say *Whaddya gonna do?*

"We weren't against you, Aldo," said Aunt Caroline. "We were actually working together for you, to give both of you a wonderful experience that kids today rarely have."

I put my hands on my hips and frowned. "So you do watch TV."

"Yes," said Uncle Odin.

"And you do use computers."

"Yes," said Aunt Caroline. "We packed all the electronics away in the attic before you arrived. Actually, I'm a technology development specialist. I sort of design computers."

"I thought you were a farm mom."

"We do live on this little farm, which has belonged to your family for generations...but both your Uncle Odin and I have office jobs, too."

"Then who does the farm chores every day?"

"Other people do a lot of the work," said Uncle Odin. "The vegetable garden, chickens, and orchard are part of a Community Supported Agriculture project. That means our neighbors work the farm in exchange for a share of the food. We board the horses for friends nearby who don't have room. And we borrowed the cows. They actually belong to the Fitschens, one field over."

My head was spinning. *What else was pretend?*

"Do you always hang your clothes outside to dry?"

"We usually use the clothes dryer," said Aunt Caroline.

Timothy came to stand beside me. "What about baling hay?" he asked.

"Someone else usually does it, but this time we took care of it ourselves," said Uncle Odin, "to give you the experience. Boy was I sore the next day."

"So <u>that's</u> why your fiddling sounded terrible!" I realized aloud. "It was part of the hoax!"

Everyone laughed except me and Timothy.

"Actually, we've all been studying the Laura Ingalls Wilder books to brush up on how an old-fashioned family behaved," said Aunt Caroline. "Fiddling seemed to be an essential activity."

"Like whittling and making butter," I said.

"Precisely!" she said.

"Square-dancing?" asked Timothy.

"We're not what you'd call regulars," said Uncle Odin.

"My cell phone?" asked Timothy.

"I installed a device that scrambled the cell phone signals unless you were in the attic," he said. "I've turned it off now."

"And <u>you two</u>," I said, pointing at Chaz and Al. "You were playing video games and computers and watching TV all week, weren't you? <u>That's</u> what was making the noises I kept hearing at night. <u>That's</u> why you were so tired in the mornings."

Chaz and Al grinned sheepishly and got cherry-Slushie red in the face.

"Charles and Almanzo Anderson! You were <u>forbidden</u> to use electronics this week!" Aunt Caroline said sternly to the twins. "I'll deal with you later."

Mom stood to hug Uncle Odin and Aunt Caroline, and her voice choked up* a little when she said, "Thank you for giving us such an amazing gift. Great-grandfather Aldo would be proud of how you're caring for the farm." Then she laughed. "Of course, he'd also be tickled by all the pranks that have been played here this week!"

Hmph. I'm not feeling <u>at all</u> tickled.

I left the house to get away from everyone and went to the chicken coop to nibble a chicken pellet or two. Sometimes a snack picks you up when you're feeling low.

I found Timothy juggling eggs. Yolky little puddles lay all around him.

"Whassup," he said.

"What's up is we got cahootsed. I don't like it."

"Yeah," he said. "Me either."

All the chickens were out at recess. During the daytime, the gate to the run is left open so they can roam freely around the farm.

I reached into the chicken feed bucket to grab a few pellets, then I sat on the bucket to watch Timothy juggle. He was trying 6. That's why there were so many smashed eggs.

When all the eggs were toast, Timothy said, "The only eggs left are Cordelia's. Let's go see if she's there."

So we snuck into the coop, and sure enough, there sat broody Cordelia. Even when all the other chickens were out having a good time, there she faithfully sat.

"Hey Cordelia," I said. "Want a pellet?" I tossed one gently to her, wondering if she'd catch it like Maxie would. She didn't. But she did stand up and kinda shuffle around for a minute, and that's when I saw that she was sitting on eggs— and baby lizards!

"Hey, her eggs are hatching," said Timothy.

"She's having geckos?" I said.

"No, those are baby chicks. They're just slimy from being born. Look."

As we inched closer, I thought Cordelia might peck out our eyeballs, but instead she strutted off for a drink of water. Sure enough, some of her eggs were cracked into little pieces, and about five weird little critters* with beaks and wings were pushing bits of shell aside and trying to stretch and stand.

By now I was kneeling next to the nest and watching right up close. The strongest chick stood and took a few steps toward me. He looked me right in the face and started to peep!

"He likes me!" I said.

"He thinks you're his mama," said Timothy.

"Nuh-uh."

"Yep. He's imprinted on you. That means you have to raise him."

"It does not." (Meanwhile, louder and louder cheeps from my newborn son.)

Thankfully Cordelia came back just in time. She hopped onto the nest and settled on top of the eggs and the babies.

"She's going to warm them up and dry them off," said Timothy.

Whew, I thought. *That was a close call.*

As we stepped out of the coop, we met up with Goosy. She was standing in the field, brushing paint on a canvas. In her painting I saw the farmhouse and the barn, the vegetable garden and the tire swing, the cows and the chickens. From where she stood, the farm did look like a painting—all reds and greens and warm browns with chickeny dots of white under a blue, blue sky.

"I hear there's been some fun on the farm this week," she said, and she laughed her Goosy belly-laugh.

"It's not funny," I said.

"That's not what I heard."

"Well, it's not <u>fair</u>," I said.

"Fair's in August," she said, and she winked at me. *Whatever that means.*

I WENT BACK TO CHECK ON GECKO-CHICK LATER AND, SURE ENOUGH, HE WAS ALL YELLOW AND FLUFFY—AND HE STARTED FOLLOWING ME AROUND! I NAMED HIM CALVIN.

FAIR'S IN AUGUST

I found out what it means: Today we got to go to the Minnesota State Fair!

What's a state fair, you ask? Welp, if you've never been to one, you've gotta go. It's a giant carnival / food court / amusement park / farm extravaganza, all rolled into one.

We drove to the Twin Cities, which is an hour-ish away from the farm, and met my other grandparents there—Grandma Ginny (of the dill pickles) and Grandpa Carl. They used to live by Chaz and Al, but they moved to Paul Bunyan land—up by a lake so big it's called Superior.

They're into helping protect places where water birds like loons and ducks hang out. They're also into square-dancing. *Ack.* We watched them and their dancing club do a demonstration at the fair, though, and it <u>was</u> pretty impressive—until I got "volunteered" to join them on stage. Sheesh.

After the dancing, Dad introduced me to the amazing world of food on a stick. Cheescake on a stick. Fried pickles on a stick. Colossal gummy bears on a stick. Pizza on a stick. Walleye fish on a stick. Even mashed potatoes on a stick! Basically, Minnesota stole my idea about toothpicked food, except they use bigger pieces of wood for the handles.

I tried a bunch of sticked foods while we checked out all the coolest fair spots: the giant slide; the life-size cow carved from butter; the colossal pumpkins; the haunted house; the reptile room—to name just a few. Timothy and

Al (turns out he's athletic) threw baseballs at a machine that clocks how many miles-per-hour you're throwing, while I went with Chaz (turns out he's not athletic—like me!) to the arcade.

I was enjoying an uber-thick, gigantic slice of chocolate-covered bacon on a stick when all of us met back up at the Miracle of Birth Center. It's this special barn where you can watch baby animals get born. Kinda gross; kinda cool. I saw baby chicks that looked just like Calvin. In one pen, a fat mama pig lounged while her little piglets slept in a heap next to her. Then one of the fair helpers lifted up a piglet and let me and Timothy and the twins pet it! I caught the guy looking askance at my bacon, and that's when I realized: piglets + pig chow + time = my favorite food. Dang. I couldn't even eat the last bite.

On the midway, we got to do the Ferris wheel and the giant swings and the octopus ride. Even the grown-ups were getting in on the action! But it wasn't until we climbed into the Tilt-a-Whirl that Timothy and I noticed the opportunity for the ultimate revenge.

Yep, I got carsick—all over my conniving* cousins.

When we got back to the farm, Mom called Mr. Mot to check on Max, and Mr. Mot told her that I should get on a computer because he had a surprise for me. Aunt Caroline helped, and guess what? I got to have a video phone call with Mr. Mot and Jack and Bee—and Max! Max licked the screen, and the humans told me how they had been in cahoots on the no-electronics scheme, too.

"Your mother suggested that we write you letters," said Mr. Mot. "She thought that in your state of digital deprivation, you might appreciate written correspondence.*"

"Yeah, when your mom told me about the no video-game thing, she said it was a secret," said Jack. "But I knew you'd figure it out the first day you were there. That's what happened, right?"

"Heh. Not so much," I said. "But having the headlamp helped. Thanks."

I told Bee all about the CSA garden and orchard and promised to bring her back some veggies in our healthy-snack traveling cooler.

"Sweet corn!" she said. "I want sweet corn!"

She's corny.* This whole week has been corny.

INTO THE SUNSET

Welp, we're finally in the car, headed for home, sweet home.

Before we left, Uncle Odin sat us all down to watch a video he'd made. Apparently, his day job involves planning and putting in sophisticated security systems for businesses. That's how the fancy video camera on the back of the attic door got there. The camera could see through Old Aldo's portrait somehow, which is what made it look like his eyes were blinking sometimes.

But that wasn't the only spy-cam Uncle Odin had installed on the farm. Just for fun, he had also put them in the chicken coop, inside and outside the barn, on the front porch, even in the woods. So the cameras had captured lots of amusing video of all of us doing silly things.

There was Dad shaking the butter jar. There was Uncle Odin screeching away on the fiddle. There was Aunt Caroline spilling wet laundry in the mud. There was Al-the-ghost running like a lunatic down the garden path. There was Mom in the attic, calling someone on her cell phone. (Hey!!!)

And there was me...lots of me...eating chicken pellets, upchucking on Mr. Ed, slipping on the butter step in nothing but cloud underwear, screaming when I saw the floating robe in the woods...you get the idea.

"You're not <u>really</u> s'posed to eat the chicken feed," said Al. "It was a joke. I pretend-ate a piece."

"Heh. I knew that," I said.

Before my family got into our minivan and she revved up her motorcycle, Goosy rounded us all up into a group hug. I was the smallest person, so I got smushed into the very middle. It was kinda hard to breathe in there, and it smelled like farmy bodies and manure, but it felt, welp, authentic.

In the midst of all the hugging and goodbying, I could swear I heard the warble of a fiddle. It sounded like the song Mom had sung for us in the chicken coop! I looked around and caught Timothy's eye. He heard it too! He pointed up at the attic window, where a shadowy figure seemed to be swaying back and forth.

I went to get Mom's attention, but Timothy stopped me. "Bye, Old Aldo," he called to the window. "See ya around!"

"Uh yeah. See ya," I added. "You've got a nice place here. Watch over Calvin for me."

The fiddle music continued as we climbed into the car, though no one else seemed to notice it. The twins handed me a few GameBoy games for the trip, and I told them they could hang out in my fort if they come to Colorado sometime.

As we pulled away, Mom sighed deeply.

"I love that farm," she said. "And I love that song." She winked at me and Timothy, then she hummed as we headed west, into the sunset.

TWIN-SPEAK

Remember how Chaz and Al kept saying weird code phrases to each other? Turns out it wasn't code—it was twin language. Apparently, lots of twins invent words that just the two of them understand. It's called cryptophasia, which means "secret language." Weird.

Here's a key I made up to the twin-speak I heard this week:

chinnel (pg. 55): random stuff

dopo me gusha, peedunkey? (pg. 40): This is from the video game *Star Wars: Demolition*, actually. Pugwis says it, and it means, "Do you feel lucky, punk?"

huppa dee (pg. 51): Prank the show-off.

huppa do (pg. 51): OK. I will.

jeeby (pg. 72): Let's pretend we're afraid.

jeeby jo (pg. 72): I think a mosquito just flew down my throat.

p.s. Did you happen to notice Chaz's crossed fingers on page 46?

"C" GALLERY

Mr. Mot used to be an English teacher. He's a word nerd, and he likes to help me use awesome words in my sketchbooks. I mark the best words with one of these: * (it's called an asterisk). When you see an * you'll know you can look here, in the Gallery, to see what the word means. If you don't know how to say some of the words, just ask Mr. Mot. Or someone you know who's like Mr. Mot. Or go to aldozelnick.com, and we'll say them for you.

cacophony (pg. 85): a super-annoying, blaring, LOUD noisiness

cagey (pg. 9): tricky and sneaky and untrustable

cahoots (pg. 72): when you team up with someone else to do something sneaky

calamine lotion (pg. 78): a pale pink liquid that smells like diapers

calculation (pg. 17): a figuring out of something

calf (pg. 102): a cow kid. (A cow kid is a calf. A goat kid is a kid. Does that mean grown-ups think people kids are like goats—or vice versa?)

calligraphy (pg. 29): some kind of fancy handwriting

calm, cool, and collected (pg. 19): a phrase you use when you want to emphasize your calm coolness

I'M SO COOL, ICE CUBES ARE JEALOUS.

cantaloupe (pg. 31): a melon with thick, spiderwebby crust on the outside and sweet, orange yumminess on the inside

Canadian bacon (pg. 85): bogus bacon. More like ham (also good, but not in the same league).

cantankerous (pg. 97): uber-grouchy and cranky

capable (pg. 119): good at doing things

canasta (pg. 95): a game that only codgers must know about, because I don't

capacious (pg. 95): really, really big and roomy. Rhymes with spacious and means the same thing, basically.

canine (pg. 95): a dog (C'mon, Mr. Mot. Just say dog.)

HEY! I GOT LEFT OUT OF THIS BOOK!

careened (pg. 82): moved so quickly that you practically tipped over. (The drawing careened onto the next page.)

144

cat's pajamas
(pg. 7): I don't get what being cool has to do with a cat wearing pajamas, but that's what this phrase means.

catapulted (pg. 83): shot with force through the air. (Hey, what if you catapulted a cat?)

carefree
(p. 94): just plain happy, with no worries

carnivore (pg. 16): people who eat meat. (I'm more of a porkivore, really, since my favorite meats are in the pork family. Or were, till I saw the piglet. Now I'm conflicted.*)

catatonic
(pg. 32): dazed, with no expression on your face because you're feeling so zombified

carsick (pg. 35): when you feel oogy and throw-uppish from being moved around

caterwauling
(pg. 80): screechy howling

145

cattywampus (pg. 116): across-from, sideways; kitty-corner (Last year in school, my desk was cattywampus from Marvin Shoemaker's. He didn't make shoes, but he did get nosebleeds all the time and stuff tissues up his nose and leave them there the entire day. So yeah.)

cauliflower (pg. 59): a white vegetable that not only looks like brain, it tastes as delicious as you'd expect brain to taste

celestial (pg. 98): in the sky

charade (pg. 94): a pretend show

charismatic (pg. 95): when you're so awesome

that everybody likes you and follows you around and does what you say. (Note to self: work on charismatic skills. Could come in handy.)

chic (pg. 136): French word that's pronounced "sheek" and means stylish

chillax (pg. 19): chill out plus relax = chillax

chipper (pg. 65): all happy and positive

chirrupy (pg. 44): sing-songy and twittery sounding, like annoyingly happy birds in cartoon princess movies

ICK!

chock-full (pg. 95): completely, tippy-top full. The box was chock-full of chalk.

CHALK

choked up (pg. 128): when you're talking and starting to cry at the same time

chortled (pg. 32): chuckled merrily

chump (pg. 123): a person who was dumb enough to let himself be tricked

ciao (pg. 24): Italian word that's pronounced "chow." It can mean hello OR goodbye, which is kind of confusing if you ask me.

clambered (pg. 24): climbed up

clandestine (pg. 43): uber-secret and sneaky

cliffhanger (pg. 119): the part of the story where you're just about to find out the big secret but the author stalls you to make the excitement last longer—like by making you look up a word in the Word Gallery

clockwise (pg. 116): in a circle, the direction clock hands move

clods (pg. 79): clumps

clomping (pg. 59): loud walking, like when you're wearing heavy boots in an echo-y hallway

clotheslined (pg. 65): when you're moving really fast and you run into something at the level of your neck. Ouch, Chaz, watch where you're going!

cockamamie (pg. 15): ridiculous and pointless (which electronics are NOT, by the way)

codger (pg. 82): a weird, old guy

coldhearted (pg. 31): when you're mean and you don't feel bad about it

collaborate (pg. 123): work together to do something good. There's a fine line between collaborating and cahootsing if you ask me.

colossal (pg. 11): supersized; humongous

commotion (pg. 43): a noisy, bothersome disturbance

companionship (pg. 95): having a friend who makes you happy just hanging out with him

compelling (pg. 93): irresistibly powerful

competitive (pg. 8, 56): when you care about winning more than almost anything

comprehended (pg. 39): understood

condiment (pg. 80): a flavorful sauce you put on top of boring food to make it taste yummier

confident (pg. 7): when you're pretty sure of something. For example, ketchup is America's favorite sauce, so ketchup is a charismatic, confident condiment.

I RULE!

conflicted (pg. 145): when you're ambivalent about something, which means you feel two ways about it. Like, I mostly feel excited about bacon, but now a drop of guilt has been stirred into my excitement.

confront (pg. 90): when you bravely come face-to-face with something or someone to say you don't agree

conked out (pg. 41): deep asleep

conniption (pg. 8, 11): a fit; a tantrum

conniving (pg. 136): sneakily working together

conquered (pg. 13): beat; defeated

considerate (pg. 56): kind; nice

consonants (pg. 36): all the letters of the alphabet that aren't a, e, i, o, and u

conspiracy (pg. 26): when people are working together in a secret way to trick or control other people

contemporary (pg. 123): now-ish; present-day

contender (pg. 18): someone who's good enough to win. Usually pronounced con-ten-duh for some reason.

contribute (pg. 12): give to something that helps people besides you

convened (pg. 63): got together; met

conveniences (pg. 31): things that make life easier and better

copacetic (pg. 45): when everything's cool and right with the world

copious (pg. 115): lots of. I like copious bacon.

copycat (pg. 73): someone who does exactly what someone else is doing

copyright (pg. 31): a legal way to prove you invented an idea

cordially (pg. 95): with niceness

corny (pg. 138): silly in an obvious way

correspondence (pg. 137): good old-fashioned letter-writing

cosmic (pg. 40): from outerspace

could eat a horse (pg. 41): an expression that means you're really, really hungry—so hungry you could eat a large, scary land mammal with hooves (weird)

courageously (pg. 108): done with braveness

cowlick (pg. 47): the place where your hair sticks up no matter how much you wet it down

cows come home (pg. 112): As in, "till the cows come home." This saying means "all day long." Larry, Moe, and Curly don't ever leave home, so I don't get it.

cozied (pg. 54): snuggled up against

cranky (pg. 102): in a bad mood—and showing it

crestfallen (pg. 45): sad; disappointed

critters (pg. 130): little country animals

crop circles (pg. 119): supposedly aliens come to farms and make big patterns in the fields at night when everyone is sleeping. Why? No idea.

cruel (pg. 17): mean on purpose. A lot like coldhearted.*

C U L8R (pg. 43): see you later

curmudgeonly (pg. 115): a curmudgeon is someone who always looks at the negative side of things and seems grouchy and unhappy. I'm not curmudgeonly. I'm just realistic!

cuzzes (pg. 56): cousins

"I LOST MY TOOTHPASTE," SHE SAID, CRESTFALLEN.

WHAT IF IT FELL OUT THE WINDOW? HOW WILL I EVER BRUSH MY TEETH?

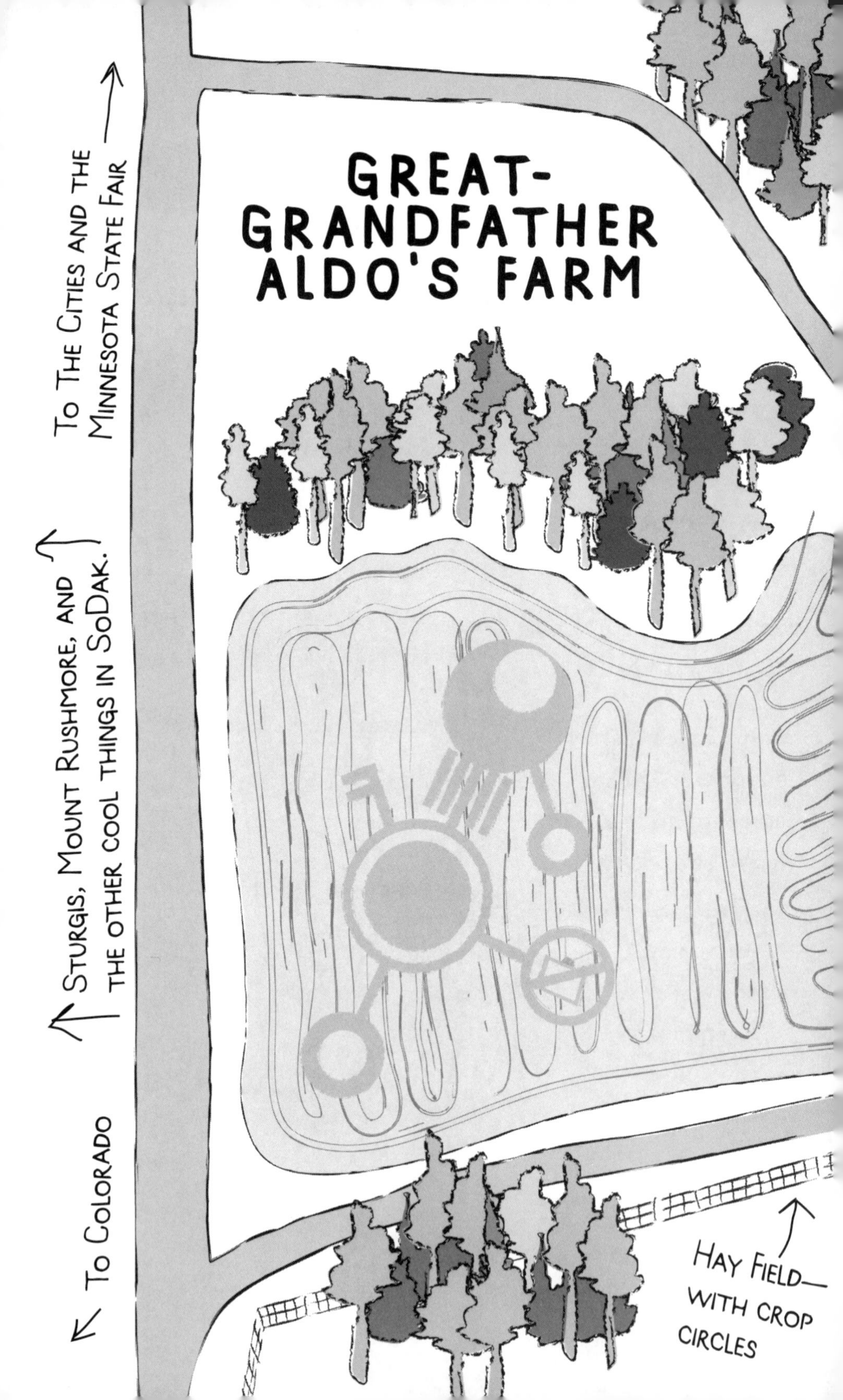
GREAT-GRANDFATHER ALDO'S FARM
TO THE CITIES AND THE MINNESOTA STATE FAIR
STURGIS, MOUNT RUSHMORE, AND THE OTHER COOL THINGS IN SODAK.
TO COLORADO
HAY FIELD— WITH CROP CIRCLES

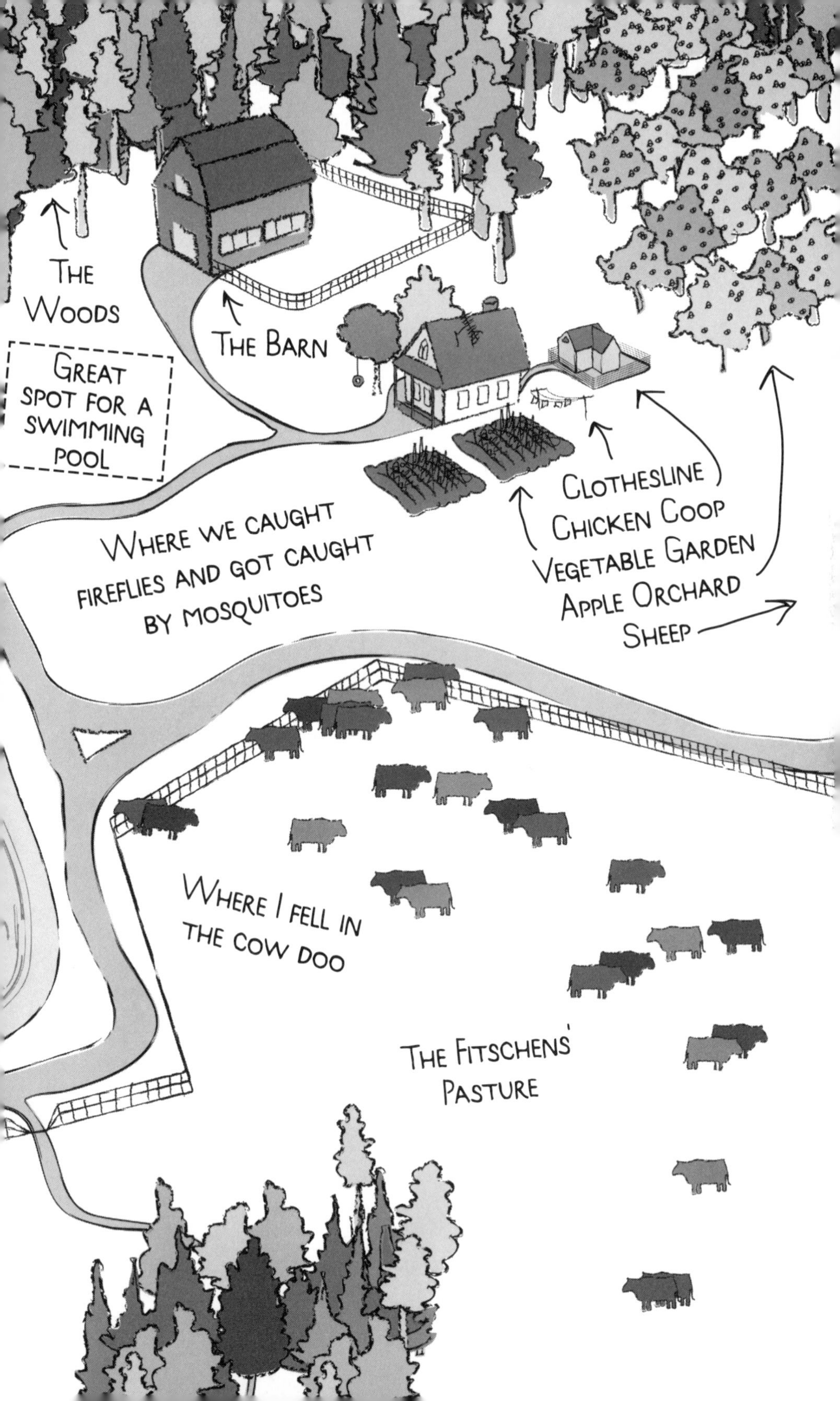
The Woods
The Barn
Great spot for a swimming pool
Where we caught fireflies and got caught by mosquitoes
Clothesline
Chicken Coop
Vegetable Garden
Apple Orchard
Sheep
Where I fell in the cow doo
The Fitschens' Pasture

ABOUT THE *award-winning* ALDO ZELNICK
COMIC NOVEL SERIES

The Aldo Zelnick comic novels are an alphabetical series for middle-grade readers aged 7-13. Rabid and reluctant readers alike enjoy the intelligent humor and drawings as well as the action-packed stories. They've been called vitamin-fortified *Wimpy Kids*.

NOW AVAILABLE!

160 pages | Hardcover
ISBN: 978-1-934649-04-6
$12.95

Part comic romps, part mysteries, and part sesquipedalian-fests (ask Mr. Mot), they're beloved by parents, teachers, and librarians as much as kids.

Artsy-Fartsy introduces ten-year-old Aldo, the star and narrator of the entire series, who lives with his family in Colorado. He's not athletic like his older brother, he's not a rock hound like his best friend, but he does like bacon. And when his artist grandmother, Goosy, gives him a sketchbook to "record all his artsy-fartsy ideas" during summer vacation, it turns out Aldo is a pretty good cartoonist.

In addition to an engaging cartoon story, each book in the series includes an illustrated glossary of fun and challenging words used throughout the book, such as *absurd, abominable*, and *audacious* in *Artsy-Fartsy* and *brazen, behemoth*, and *boisterous* in *Bogus*.

BOGUS

NOW AVAILABLE!

In this second book in the award-winning Aldo Zelnick comic novel series, Aldo and his best friend, Jack, find a diamond ring, which Aldo is sure is bogus—even though Jack—the rock hound!—believes it's real. Aldo loses then finds then loses the ring again, and bedlam ensues. Where will the ring turn up, and who will reap the rewards?

160 pages | Hardcover | ISBN 978-1-934649-06-0 | $12.95

DUMBSTRUCK

COMING OCTOBER 2011

Embarrassed about his artistic abilities, Aldo has always underplayed his talent at school. When he starts 5th grade and meets his cute new art teacher, though, he finds himself doing crazy things, like losing the ability to speak when she's around, giving up recess to clean paintbrushes, and working harder than he's ever worked at anything in a daring attempt to win the school art contest.

160 pages | Hardcover | ISBN 978-1-934649-16-9 | $12.95

EGGHEAD

COMING MAY 2012

It's October, and Aldo thinks he's Einstein. Gloating over his exemplary first-quarter grades and test scores, he even decides to dress as the iconic scientist for Halloween. But his bubble bursts when he realizes he's not excelling in one class, Español, and that the consequences may be more hurtful than a bad grade on a report card. Is Aldo's friendship with his bilingual best friend, Jack, at stake?

160 pages | Hardcover | ISBN 978-1-934649-17-6 | $12.95

BAILIWICK PRESS

www.bailiwickpress.com | www.aldozelnick.com

ACKNOWLEDGMENTS

*"It is the sweet, simple things of life
which are the real ones after all."*

— Laura Ingalls Wilder

As we write this, Aldo has wormed his way into the hearts and bookshelves of thousands of children across the United States (and even, we're told, Canada, England, China, Indonesia, and New Zealand!). You'll find him in your neighborhood bookstore, online retailer, and local library. For us, knowing that kids are enjoying reading is the sweet, simple thing.

Many colleagues and cohorts were in cahoots with us on this one. Thanks to: the crackerjack team at Independent Publishers Group, who champion Aldo everywhere, every day; coolest-ever interns Beth, Bonnie, and Chris, who delight in comma conversations (and crassness) as much as we do; the Slow Sanders, for criticism beyond compare; and Launie, whose consummate design deserves its own Caldecott. Our families indulge the long work hours these (deceivingly simple) books require, and for that we're ever-so-grateful. Finally, thank you to Aldo's Angels, whose constancy confounds us.

"An alphabetical series?" we've been asked over and over. "Won't you run out of ideas?" Welp, who knows what the future holds, but as we begin *Dumbstruck*, we're happy to report that the idea wellspring overflows and makes us laugh out loud every single day.

Barbara Anderson

Carol & Wes Baker

Butch Byram

Annie Dahlquist

Michael & Pam Dobrowski

Leigh Waller Fitschen

Sawyer & Fielding Gray (and Chris & Sarah)

Teresa Funke

Roy Griffin

Calvin Halvorson & Bennett Zent (and Chet)

Oliver Harrison (and Matthew & Erin)

Terry & Theresa Harrison

Richard & Peggy Hohm

Chris Hutchinson

IB PAB (Jana Knezovich, Linda Mahan, Starr Teague & Jacki Witlen)

Anne Keasling

Vicki & Bill Krug

Tutu, Grant, Cole, & Iris Ludwin

Annette & Tom Lynch

Kristin & Henry Mouton

The Motz & Scripps families (McCale, Alaina & Caden)

Jackie O'Hara & Erin Rogers

Betty Oceanak

David Orphanides

Alveta Petersen

Jackie Peterson

Ryan Petros

Terri Berryman Rosen

Roberta Satterfield

John Schiller & Suzanne Holm

Slow Sand Writers Society

Barb & Steve Spanjer

Dana Spanjer

Vince & Adrianne Tranchitella

Laura White Welciek

Halo There! If you're an Aldo Zelnick fan, e-mail info@bailiwickpress.com and ask for details about becoming an Aldo's Angel. Angels receive special opportunities such as pre-publication discounts, free shipping, naming rights, and listing in the acknowledgments (especially fun for kids).

VISIT ALDOZELNICK.COM TO...

- learn more about upcoming books in the series.
- hear how to pronounce the Gallery words.
- see the characters in full color.
- download coloring pages and learn more about them.
- suggest a word for an upcoming book.
- see Karla and Kendra's appearance schedule or invite them to your school, bookstore, or event.
- sign up for our e-mail list.